"I was empty, too, Caden."

"By choice, Emma."

True again. She swallowed hard and reached for him, half afraid that he'd step away from her, leaving her shattered just to teach her a lesson.

She hadn't come here for this, at least not consciously. But maybe this was what had been driving her since she got home. The need to touch him and be touched. To remember what it felt like to be so alive that she practically glowed.

Emma moved up to him and kept her gaze locked with his. Laying both hands on his shoulders, she looked into his lake-blue eyes and said, "We've been empty too long, Caden. Fill me up. Fill us both."

"Damn you for leaving, Emma," he murmured, his gaze moving over her face, then coming back to look deeply into hers. "And damn you for coming back."

Then he grabbed her, pulled her in close and bent his head to hers.

Dear Reader,

I love a cowboy. Of course, most of us can say that, right? In *Red Hot Rancher*, you'll meet Caden Hale, a rich, gorgeous cowboy, and Emma Williams, the woman who actually walked away from him.

Caden and Emma had been a couple since high school and they shared lots of big, beautiful plans for the future. But then Emma realized that if she didn't leave home and try to make her own dreams come true, she'd never truly be happy—no matter how much she loved Caden.

She's gone five years, and when she comes back, she has to earn her place and the trust of everyone she loves.

Caden and Emma have a lot of things to face, but when there's love, there's always a chance.

I hope you enjoy this story as much as I did! Please visit me on Facebook to let me know what you think!

Until next time,

Maureen Child

MAUREEN CHILD

———

RED HOT RANCHER

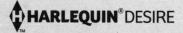

HARLEQUIN® DESIRE

Recycling programs
for this product may
not exist in your area.

ISBN-13: 978-1-335-60374-6

Red Hot Rancher

Copyright © 2019 by Maureen Child

Printed in U.S.A.

www.Harlequin.com

Maureen Child writes for the Harlequin Desire line and can't imagine a better job. A seven-time finalist for a prestigious Romance Writers of America RITA® Award, Maureen is the author of more than one hundred romance novels. Her books regularly appear on bestseller lists and have won several awards, including a Prism Award, a National Readers' Choice Award, a Colorado Romance Writers Award of Excellence and a Golden Quill Award. She is a native Californian but has recently moved to the mountains of Utah.

Books by Maureen Child

Harlequin Desire

The Baby Inheritance
Maid Under the Mistletoe
The Tycoon's Secret Child
A Texas-Sized Secret
Little Secrets: His Unexpected Heir
Rich Rancher's Redemption
Billionaire's Bargain
Tempt Me in Vegas
Bombshell for the Boss
Red Hot Rancher

Texas Cattleman's Club: Houston

Wild Ride Rancher

Visit her Author Profile page at Harlequin.com, or maureenchild.com, for more titles.

You can find Maureen Child on Facebook, along with other Harlequin Desire authors, at Facebook.com/HarlequinDesireAuthors!

To my kids,
Jason and Sarah,
who have added so much love and
laughter to our lives.
I wouldn't have missed a minute of it.

One

"She's back."

"She *who*?" Caden Hale looked up at his foreman, Jack Franklin. No one knew him better than Jack, which was why Caden was surprised to see the man now.

Everyone on the ranch knew not to disturb Caden when he was engulfed by the dreaded paperwork needed to keep the Double H ranch running. Caden would much rather be out in the corral or riding fence-line, checking for breaks. Hell, to be honest, he'd rather be in the stables, mucking out stalls. But at least once a week, he was forced to sentence himself to hours behind the desk that had once been his father's.

Jack stood opposite that desk now and the foreman's expression was a weird mixture of dread and shock. Caden braced himself, leaning back in the chair, tapping one finger against the desktop.

Caden didn't have a clue who could have put that look on his oldest friend's face. He and Jack had been pals since grade school and when Caden took over the family ranch ten years ago, Jack had come on board, too. Usually, the man was unshakable. Not today.

"Come on, Jack. What's going on? You look like somebody died."

"Not yet," his friend muttered, then swept off his Stetson, curled his fingers around the brim and tapped the hat against his upper thigh.

Caden straightened in the chair, leaned both forearms on the desk and stared at his friend. "Just spit it out. Who the hell are you talking about and why should I care?"

"You shouldn't care," Jack said. "But you will."

"Enough. Just tell me."

"It's Emma, Caden," Jack told him flatly. "Emma Williams is back."

And just like that, the day went from annoying to a crap-fest. Caden's chest was tight, and he didn't even notice how hard he was clenching his teeth until his jaw ached in response. Deliberately, he took a long, deep breath and willed the sudden tension in his body to drain away.

Damned if he'd let a woman he hadn't seen or spoken to in five long years get under his skin. And yet, he had to admit, just the mention of her name had done it. Caden closed his eyes briefly to fight the wave of tangled emotions rising up inside him. Anger and betrayal were tied for first place, but the rest weren't far behind. Lust, the remnants of a love he thought would live forever and just enough pleasure to worry him.

Emma was back.

Why? For how long?

And damn it, why did he care? He hadn't spoken to her in five years. She'd tried to call a few times, but he'd never answered. Why the hell should he?

"Did you see her?" he finally asked.

"No," Jack said with a sharp shake of his head. "Gwen did. She was in town this morning, getting some groceries. Saw Emma wandering the aisles. Caden," he added, "she had a baby with her."

Another sucker punch and now breathing was becoming a hell of a lot harder than it should have been. A *baby*? She'd had a baby while she was gone? With who? Was the baby's father here with them? "Damn it."

"Yeah," Jack said. "When Gwen told me I knew this wasn't going to go well."

"Good call."

Caden exhaled roughly, hoping to ease the raging tide of conflicting emotions rising inside him.

Yeah, he was still furious over how Emma had ended things between them, but through it all, there was a hot, thick wave of need he'd never been able to shake. Just thinking about Emma Williams was enough to make his body hard as stone and his mind an empty cavern. Which was why, he reminded himself, he'd tried to avoid all thought of her for the past five years. It was only in his dreams that she came back to haunt him. Every damn night.

"Did Gwen talk to her?" Jack's wife knew everything that had happened between Caden and Emma. Hell, everyone for miles around knew the story. It's what happened in a small town.

Cache, Montana, had a population that hovered around five thousand. If you needed a big city once in a while, Kalispell was only thirty miles away. But Cache was large enough for Caden. It had everything he needed. There were stores and schools and Main Street was dotted with buildings that were built more than a hundred years ago. It was small, but it was his. A tiny town, where everyone felt free to share their opinion on just about anything.

"Yeah." Jack pushed one hand through his hair. "She says Emma got home last night. Didn't tell anyone she was coming…"

Which explained why Emma's sister Gracie hadn't said anything about this to Caden when he saw her yesterday. And he was willing to bet that Gracie was no happier about this than he was.

"Says she's home to stay. She's done with Hollywood."

"Is that right?" Teeth clenched, he thought about what this would mean for him. He'd have to see her all the damn time now. The town would resurrect old stories and he'd catch people watching him with mocking eyes—or worse yet, sympathy.

Still, she'd left once before. Why should he believe that she would stay now?

"Caden," Jack advised, "just let it be."

He shot a look at his oldest friend. Jack looked worried but he couldn't help the man with that. If Emma was home, then he was going to face her and get a few things out in the open. "Not going to happen. She's back and we're going to talk. Set things straight right away."

"What's left to set straight? You guys ended it five years ago."

"*She* ended it," Caden reminded the other man. "Now it's *my* turn."

"What exactly is your problem, Gracie?" Emma Williams caught her younger sister's arm to stop her before she could flounce out of the room Emma had just entered.

The living room was as it had always been. Wide windows overlooking the front yard and the long driveway leading up to the Williams' ranch. Furniture chosen for its comfort rather than style and now threadbare rugs that her mother had hooked before Emma was born. Watery October sunlight pushed its way through the grime on the windows and spotlighted dust motes floating in the still air.

Gracie yanked her arm free. "You, Em. You're my problem."

Her sister had been avoiding her since the night before, when Emma had walked into the house as if she'd been gone an hour instead of five years.

"How?" Emma threw both hands high. "I just got home last night."

"Exactly." Gracie tossed her short, curly hair back from her face. "You've been gone a long time, Emma. Then you show up and we're all supposed to act like you've been here all along? Like nothing's changed? Like the ranch isn't falling apart and Dad has hardly gotten out of bed in the last year?"

Gracie's green eyes, so much like Emma's own, were flashing with fury, and at least, Emma told herself, that was honest. Since the night before, Gracie had been shut down, refusing to speak to her. Well, angry shouts were at least communication of a sort.

And everything her sister was saying jabbed at her like hot needles. She'd had time to look around the ranch this morning and Gracie was right. The place looked as though it was struggling and their father was grayer and slower then she remembered. But even as she felt that quick jolt of guilt, she defended herself.

"You never told me Dad was sick," she countered. And worry twisted with guilt inside her.

"He wasn't," her sister retorted. "Isn't. He just gave up. Because *you* walked away."

That hurt and she really hoped it wasn't true. But it felt true and Emma's pain rose up to choke her. She hadn't meant to leave a trail of destruction in her wake when she left. Hadn't meant a lot of things. And that changed nothing. "You should have told me."

"In an email?" Gracie asked hotly. "Or one of your famous two-minute phone calls? Yeah, lots of time for a chat then, huh, Em?"

More guilt. Great.

"You can't lay this all on me, Gracie," Emma argued. "You were here. You knew what was happening."

"And couldn't change it," her sister said as tears filled her eyes. She took a deep breath, blinked the tears away and when she spoke again, her voice was low, but controlled. "I was trying to hold the ranch together and all Dad could do was worry about you. 'All alone in California.' While I was all alone right here."

Stung, Emma swayed at the impact of her sister's words. It was true that she hadn't thought about what would happen here at home when she left. Maybe she hadn't *allowed* herself to think of it.

Five years ago, she'd seen her future laid out

in front of her and something inside her had just *snapped*. She'd had to go. Had to *try*.

"Gracie…" She didn't know what she might have said, but it didn't matter when her sister cut her off.

"Don't say you're sorry. It doesn't matter and besides, you're really not." She swiped away a solitary angry tear. "You did what you wanted to do. Just like you always have."

For the first time in this conversation, Emma felt a quick blast of anger. She was willing to take a little bit of bitterness from her sister, but damned if she'd stand there and be a target for whatever Gracie wanted to throw at her.

"Seriously? What the hell is that supposed to mean?" Emma moved in closer, kept her voice low so their father wouldn't overhear them. "When Mom died, who was it who held this place together, taking care of you and Dad? Besides, you *don't* do what you want? Since when? You stole Dad's truck for a joyride, remember? And, you ditched school and hitched a ride to a concert in Billings—"

"When I was a kid," Gracie cut her off. "Don't have any new stories to tell, though, do you, Em? Because you weren't *here*."

This was getting old, fast. "A lot of people leave home, Gracie."

"Most of them at least visit."

"If they can *afford it*," Emma argued.

"You were on TV," Gracie shot back.

"For one season," Emma reminded her and on one level, she couldn't believe they were having this argument. God, she hadn't even been home for twenty-four hours.

Apparently Thomas Wolfe was wrong. You *could* go home again, you just couldn't make anyone happy to see you.

For some reason, Emma had expected it to be easier to slide back into her old life. While she was in Hollywood, this ranch, her family, had become her mental security blanket. When she was worried or scared or whatever, she'd close her eyes and let her memories soothe her.

This was *home*. It was the one place she'd told herself that was there, waiting for her if the world turned on her. She'd always told herself that she could go home if her dreams crashed and burned. But home wasn't what it had been when she left five years ago. Now that she was back in Cache, she had to admit that it wasn't what she'd remembered. What she'd hoped to find. But even as that thought settled in her mind, Emma wondered if that was true. Maybe it wasn't home that had changed, after all. It was *her*.

But how could she not? So much had happened to her in California that Montana had begun to seem like a dream world to her. She'd written and emailed and video chatted, but the longer she was away, the bigger the chasm between her and her family had grown. And how could it have been different, when she wasn't really telling them what her life was like in California? She didn't want them worried about her making rent on that dumpy little apartment in Hollywood. Didn't want them knowing that she was hungry often and anxious all the time. So she'd been bright and happy and brief in those calls that had become less and less frequent.

Her father, Frank, had always been happy to hear from her. But Gracie had slowly shut down, pulled away. And now her little sister could barely stand to be in the same room with her.

And maybe she had it coming. Emma's world was now divided into two separate entities. Before she left Montana and *now.* She preferred the before because dealing with the now was harder than anything she'd ever done. *Now* meant she had a sick father, a sister who hated her and a baby who depended on her.

What felt like boulders dropped onto Emma's shoulders and she almost sagged under the emotional weight of it all. But the truth was, none of those burdens were as crushing as the knowledge that she still had to see Caden again. And everything in her was torn.

It had been five years since she'd seen him and five minutes since she'd thought of him. He'd been in her mind forever. Since the moment they'd met in high school, Caden Hale was all she'd been able to see. All she'd *wanted* to see. Until the night he had laid out their future together. Marriage, kids, the ranch, everything they used to talk about. Everything that Emma had come to believe was somehow *destined*.

But that same night, it had become clear to her that if she stayed in Montana with him and never tried to chase down her own dreams, she'd end up resenting him and hating herself. So she'd left. Walked away. And she had the feeling he'd be even less happy to see her than Gracie was.

Since the evening before, when she'd walked in the door of her family home, Emma had been dreading and anticipating the moment when she'd face *him* again.

"Emma! Come on in here." Her father's voice splintered her thoughts and dragged her back to the moment.

"Coming, Dad!"

"Bring a bottle," he shouted, "I think my granddaughter's getting hungry!"

Emma frowned as one more weight settled on her shoulders, but she told herself that was a problem for another day. She looked at her sister and said, "We'll finish this later."

"Oh," Gracie told her, "we're finished."

Taking a breath, hoping for patience, Emma headed to the kitchen.

The drive from the Double H ranch to the Williamses' place only took about twenty minutes. Once upon a time, he and Emma had talked about one day cutting a road directly across their adjoining fields, to directly link the ranches. But that, like so many other things, had never happened.

At any other time, Caden might have noticed the fall colors erupting on the trees lining the wide road. But now, all he could see were the images replaying in his mind, of Emma's eyes the night she said goodbye.

"I have to go, Caden," she said plaintively, trying to make him understand. "I have to try. I can't do what my mom did. She gave up on her dreams. You remember what a great singer she was, right?"

"I do, but—"

"She never did anything with it and before she died, she told me that was her one regret. That she'd never found out if she could make it or not."

Panic was rising in his chest, but Caden fought it down. He and Emma had been together a long time. He'd always believed that they were working toward the same goals. This had come out of nowhere for him and he didn't know what the hell to think. "What about the dream of building up my family ranch?"

"That's your dream, Caden," she said simply and tore a hole in his heart.

That was a slap. She'd had plenty of ideas, had jumped in enthusiastically with plans. "We've been talking about this for years," he reminded her. "We were going to do it together. Create something special."

"I know." She touched him and her hand on his arm was like a fire that was bone chilling. *"But this is important to me, too, Caden. I have to find out if I'm good enough."*

Couldn't she see that she'd never be as important in Hollywood as she was right here? To him?

"So you're just leaving."

"You could come with me..."

He laughed at her. "I can't leave."

"And I can't stay," she said. *"If I don't go now, neither one of us will be happy."*

He cut off the memories and buried them under a layer of fury. She'd made it seem like she was doing him a favor by walking away. As if the dreams they'd forged together for years hadn't been as important as the ones she'd nurtured all to herself.

Well, she'd ripped his heart out that night and he'd had to shut himself down to get through it. But he had. He'd made a damn good life without Emma and it was only going to get better. And once he'd faced her and had his say, he could get back to it.

When he steered his top-of-the-line, black Dodge Ram truck up the drive to her father's ranch, he noted the peeling paint on the fence rails and the weeds choking out the front flower bed. The Williams place had been slowly going to hell since Emma left. Just another black mark against her.

Frank Williams had pretty much given up when his oldest girl had run off to Hollywood. He'd expected her to take over, to merge their ranch with Caden's as they'd always planned.

Emma had torn up a lot of dreams when she left to find her own.

Still, Caden felt a pang of guilt. He should make more time to check in on Frank and do what he could to help out. Frowning to himself, he made a mental note to send a few of his ranch hands over in a day or two to paint the corral fence. Get it done before winter, he told himself, or the damn wood would rot and warp and the whole fence would have to be replaced.

"The perfect metaphor," he muttered. When Emma left, they'd all had to rebuild. She'd taken off to chase a dream and left the rest of them wondering what the hell had happened. Now she was back.

With a baby.

He parked the truck, turned off the engine and just sat there for a minute, staring at the house where he'd spent so much of his life. It was old and sturdy, yellow, with white trim because that's how Emma's mother had liked it best. There was a big front porch and a second story where the bedrooms were. He knew this house as well as he knew his own.

He and Emma had been a couple since the year she was a freshman in high school. He'd been a "manly" junior and took substantial mocking from his friends for being interested in a "kid," but he hadn't cared.

Emma was all he'd been able to see back then and until the night she'd walked away, that hadn't changed. But things were different now. Emma had left once before. Why should he believe she was here to stay *now*? No, what was between them had curled up and died five years ago.

Yet even as that thought rose up in his mind, his body was tightening at the prospect of being near her again.

While he sat there, watching the house, the front door flew open and Gracie, Emma's younger sister, raced toward him. Caden got out of the truck in time to catch her when Gracie threw herself at him.

"I can't believe this," she muttered against his chest. "She just showed up last night like it was *nothing* and we're supposed to be happy she's here." She pulled her head back and glared up at him. "I'm not. I'm furious."

At twenty-five, Gracie was a beauty, with short, curly brown hair and green eyes a shade paler than her sister's. He'd been a big brother to Gracie all their lives and he could see that there was pain as well as fury in her eyes.

He knew how she felt. "Gwen ran into her at the market this morning. Said she's come back to stay."

Gracie let him go, took a step back and swiped a solitary tear off her cheek. "That's what she says, but why should we believe her? She left before, didn't she?"

He didn't know if it was good or bad that Gracie was pretty much echoing his own thoughts on the matter.

"Dad's happy to see her anyway." She shoved her hands into her jeans pockets and tossed her windblown hair off her forehead. "He actually got out of bed this morning."

That was news. Frank had given up on life about a year after Emma left. Little by little, he'd withdrawn more and more from everyday life. He'd started out hoping Emma would see she'd made a mistake and come running home. But finally, the older man had realized that his girl was probably gone forever and all the life in him had just drained away. Not even Gracie had been able to coax him out of the depression he'd dropped into.

If Emma left again, it'd probably kill her father this time.

"She can't be here, Caden," Gracie was saying. "What if she finds out? She'll tell Dad and then—"

"*You* should tell your dad," Caden whispered. He was the only person Gracie had trusted with her secrets and he'd never betray her. But he did think she was handling them all wrong and didn't mind saying so.

"I can't," she said, shaking her head. "Especially not now."

"Hello, Caden."

Just like that, everything in him went still and cold. He hadn't heard that low-pitched, sultry voice in too damn long, but it had the same effect on him it always had. He turned to look, saw Emma standing in the open doorway and his mouth went dry. His jeans were suddenly too tight and drawing a breath seemed near impossible.

The last time he'd seen her was on his television screen. Emma had been starring in a vapid, ridiculous sitcom, and as hard as it had been for Caden to admit, she had been really good in it. So good, he'd watched the show exactly once, got stinking drunk and never turned the damn TV on again. She'd left him for Hollywood and it burned his ass that she'd done well.

Now she was back, and why did she have to look so damn tempting?

Her dark brown hair was longer, falling well past her shoulders now, in the wild, thick curls she'd always hated. She wore a long-sleeved red flannel shirt and a pair of black jeans that hugged her hips and long, shapely legs. Her old boots completed the outfit and somehow it felt to Caden as if she'd donned a costume to fit in.

Maybe the Hollywood Emma was the real person now and this woman in front of him was the one acting out a part.

And as much as he wanted her, Caden braced himself against old emotions, desires and faced her now with the cold, empty memories flooding his mind. Her greenish-gold eyes were still as clear and beautiful as ever, but as he met her gaze, Caden saw secrets there. Something he'd never seen before.

He didn't like it.

"You're not going to say hello?" she asked.

The voice that had haunted his dreams. The woman who had haunted *everything* in his life. Caden felt a sharp stab of betrayal. She'd walked out on him five years ago and never looked back. Now she said hello like nothing had changed between them? Were they supposed to go have a drink? Catch up on old times? Maybe she'd ask him to babysit. Well, screw that.

Beside him, Gracie had a death grip on his arm, her fingers digging into his skin right through the fabric of his heavy brown coat. Reminding him where his loyalties lay now. Gracie had stayed. Had taken care of everything that Emma had walked away from. So he'd stand with her against the woman who had left them both.

"What're you doing here, Emma?"

She lifted her chin, kept her gaze fixed on his and said simply, "This is my home."

"Not for five years."

She chewed at her bottom lip and that action tugged at something inside him, too. Heat bubbled in his gut but Caden ignored it.

"I'm back now," Emma told him. "I'm not leaving again."

"Is that right?" He didn't believe her.

"It is. I'm done with Hollywood." Her chin was still lifted in self-defense mode.

She'd had success, though he didn't want to admit it. So what had changed her mind? What had chased her home? And why the hell did he still care after all this time?

"What changed?" he asked, before he could stop himself.

"I guess I did," she said.

He nodded. "Right. You changed five years ago. And now you've changed again. When's the next change coming?"

"There won't be one."

"Don't believe her," Gracie murmured.

"Oh, I don't," Caden assured her and had the satisfaction of seeing Emma's eyes flash. Anger? Insult? Didn't matter which. As long as she knew where he stood.

Even knowing he couldn't trust her didn't stop Caden from wanting her with a bone-deep desire that had never really left him. "Why don't you go inside, Gracie? I want to talk to Emma."

She gave him a long, speculative look, then did as he asked, skirting past her sister still standing in the doorway.

"Wow." Emma's gaze locked on him. "You and Gracie must be really close these days. She's taking orders from you now?"

"It wasn't an order," he told her. "It was a request."

"That she hopped to fulfill." Tipping her head to

one side, she kept her eyes on him. "What's going on between you two?"

Caden stared right back, and folded his arms across his chest. He hadn't missed the temper in her tone. "You don't get to ask that question, Emma. It's none of your business."

"She's my sister."

He laughed shortly. "You've been gone for years, Emma. All of a sudden now, you're sisters?"

"I didn't leave the family, Caden," she argued and her chin lifted a little higher. "I left Montana."

"And *me*."

She took a breath, nodded and said, "Yeah. And you. But I explained why I had to go."

Anger whipped through him like a lightning bolt. "That makes it okay that you took off? As long as you 'explained'?"

She took a breath, stuffed her hands into her jeans pockets and stared at him for a long moment before asking, "What is it you want from me, Caden?"

Well, now, that was the question, wasn't it? He'd come here to have his say. To set things straight with Emma and let her know exactly where he stood. But being here, with her, was making it hard to think.

He looked her up and down, felt a stir of need and squashed it. When he held her gaze again, he leaned in and whispered, *"Absolutely nothing."*

Two

Absolutely nothing.

For the next several days, those two words echoed in Emma's brain. There was a lot to do around the ranch and yet she couldn't shake Caden's voice.

"No surprise there," she muttered as she shuffled equipment around in the tack room. Caden had never been far from her mind. Yes, she'd walked away from him, but she'd had to follow her heart, right? Fight for her dream or end up an old woman, eaten by regret.

"You'd think he'd understand that," she said tightly. "The man has a one-track mind when it comes to *his* dreams. What? I'm not allowed to chase mine? Is that it? I can only have the dreams that don't inconvenience him?"

Absolutely nothing.

But it seemed he wanted *something* from Emma's sister. Gracie had gone to Caden's place nearly every day. Why? Jealousy bristled in her chest and twisted around her heart, giving it a hard squeeze. Was Gracie sleeping with him? Had he moved from one sister to another without missing a beat? Was Gracie the one sharing in Caden's dreams now?

She had no way of knowing since her sister hadn't really spoken to her since that first day. The two of them passed each other in the house locked in a strained silence that their father was either not noticing or actively ignoring.

Frank was completely in love with baby Molly, though, and every day, he seemed to return a bit more to the man that Emma remembered. His granddaughter had given him a new lease on life, he claimed, and that worried Emma, too. There was simply too much going on. Too many things to feel. To think. To be anxious over.

Why had she ever thought that coming home would be easy?

She grabbed two shovels and slammed them into the corner. This whole ranch was a mess. The barn, the stable, the house. Oh, it was all still standing, but it looked to Emma like no one had been paying attention to what needed doing. Except Caden, apparently. A couple of men from his ranch had been over two days ago, to repaint the corral fences, and when she had told them they didn't need his help, they'd ignored her, too. Said that they took orders from Caden and if she had a problem with it, she should take it up with him.

As if she could.

So now the fences had been painted, but the grass was too high, and the railing on the wraparound porch was wobbly. And the tack room was in shambles. "There are *shelves* for God's sake. Why aren't they using them?"

Anger guided Emma as she picked up saddle soap, cloths and a million other little supplies that were tossed around. One by one, she straightened them out, lining them up on the shelves and giving it all a nod of satisfaction when she was finished. For a soul as organized as Emma, this place was torture.

"And why is there an old saddle on the desk?" she asked no one.

"It's waiting to be repaired."

Emma spun around to see her younger sister standing in the doorway. "How long's it been waiting?"

Gracie shrugged. "A few months I guess."

"Months?" Emma shook her head, exasperated at the mess and her sister's nonchalant attitude. "Why hasn't Buck fixed it?"

"Buck quit six months ago."

"What?" Buck Simpson had worked for them since Emma was a girl. He was a master at saddlery and had kept the ranch equipment in tip-top shape. "Why?"

Gracie shrugged again and leaned one shoulder against the doorjamb. "He said he was getting too old to deal with ranching in winter. He went to live with his daughter and her husband on their ranch outside Billings. It still snows, but he doesn't have to get out and work in it every day."

Another change she hadn't known about and she didn't like it. "Why didn't you tell me? You could've emailed or something."

"Yeah, because we've been so close."

Emma sighed, shoved her hands into the back pockets of her jeans and looked at the little sister who used to follow her around like a puppy. "You know, I tried to stay close. I left the ranch, I didn't leave the *family*. I wrote to you, Gracie. I called. *You* never did."

"What was I supposed to say?" Gracie countered, pushing off the doorjamb. "Happy trails? Good luck with your perfect life while I'm here trying to hold a ranch together?"

God. She would have laughed at that if she hadn't felt like screeching.

"Perfect? You think my life was perfect?" Emma actually felt her eyes roll. "Going to auditions and never getting the part? Being told that if you sleep with the producer, he'll *consider* hiring you?

"Being on your feet for a twelve-hour shift at a

restaurant because the landlord just jacked your rent higher? *Again?* Having your ass patted by an old man when you bring his lunch order?"

"Wait," Gracie said, holding up one hand and looking around the room for effect. "Let me find a tissue."

"God, you're a bitch."

"Said the queen bitch of the universe."

Frustration rippled through her. She kept trying and kept getting shut down. Her life in Hollywood hadn't been *anyone's* idea of a dream and there was plenty more that she wasn't telling Gracie. Dark, hard things that she'd never told anyone and wouldn't use to get a glimmer of sympathy now.

"What the hell, Gracie?" Emma threw her hands up, faced her sister and demanded, "What is going on with you? This isn't all about me moving to California. You can't be this mad about me being gone for a few years. There's something else going on."

Gracie's features tightened, then went deliberately blank. "You don't know me, Emma. Not anymore. And just so you know? Everything else is fine. Just stop expecting me to be happy to have you home."

"You didn't want me leaving and now you don't want me here." Emma shook her head, then tossed her hair back behind her shoulders. "What the hell *do* you want?"

For just a split second, something flashed in Gracie's eyes, but it was gone an instant later. Emma had the distinct feeling she'd almost reached the real Gracie. The little sister she'd missed for so long.

"Nothing," Gracie said. "Look. I only came out here to tell you your daughter woke up. She's crying."

Emma drew her head back as if she'd been slapped. "And you couldn't pick her up?"

For a second, her sister's eyes shone with shame, but it didn't last long. Defiant, she lifted her chin. "I'm not your babysitter, Em. And neither is Dad."

Emma gave her a hard look. "I didn't say you were. And Dad takes care of her because he *wants* to. I haven't heard him complain about Molly."

"Of course not." Gracie took a breath and lifted one hand to push her hair back from her face. "He'd never say anything to you. You think he wants to risk you leaving again?"

"I told you. And him. I'm not leaving."

"And we should believe you," Gracie said wryly, quirking a brow.

"Damn it, Gracie, is it going to be like this between us all the time now?"

"I don't know. If it is, will you leave?"

"No."

"We'll see, won't we," Gracie said, then turned away before Emma could speak. The anger and hurt in her sister's eyes was impossible to miss.

"Wow. Welcome home, Emma."

"Right. I'll get the balloons." Gracie turned on her heel, then looked back over her shoulder. "By the way, the vet's coming over later. I'd appreciate it if you'd leave us alone."

She was gone before Emma could respond and maybe it was just as well. These "conversations" with Gracie were exhausting and sort of circular. No matter which direction they went, it eventually returned to *you left us*. And there was no argument to that because Emma had left her old life behind to try for something else. Something she'd dreamed of doing since she was a kid. No one seemed to understand that and for the millionth time, Emma found herself wishing her mom were still alive. Maggie Williams would have understood.

Emma fumed for another minute or two. Just long enough to make sure she wouldn't have to walk alongside Gracie back to the house. She'd had no idea when she left Montana that she would completely shatter the relationship she had with her sister. Emma was five years older than her sister and so she'd always looked after Gracie—especially since their mother died when Gracie was fourteen. And now it felt as if they were armed camps on opposite sides of a battle.

She blew out a breath, finished organizing the shelves and then swept the floor, focusing the burning energy inside toward getting *something* in her life straightened out. Coming home was turning into a big-scale drama. Her father was deteriorating, her sister was furious and her old boyfriend could barely stand to look at her. If she'd had the energy, Emma might have thrown herself a little pity party. But since she didn't, she headed for the house and the baby girl who needed her instead.

Molly was nearly five months old and her personality was, thank God, happy. The tiny girl welcomed everyone with a toothless smile and only cried when she was hungry or wet. You just couldn't ask for much more than that. Having Molly in her life had been a surprise, but Emma was determined to protect that baby girl. To give Molly the kind of life she'd had, growing up.

Which was the main reason she was back in Montana taking a mountain of crap from everyone.

She found her father and Molly in the living room. The baby was on his lap, laughing as Frank made silly faces. Was it her imagination, or did her dad look better today than he had when she'd arrived just a few days before? His eyes were brighter, his hair was combed and he'd shaved. All good signs that Gracie hadn't bothered to mention. Plus, her little sister had made it sound as if Frank was aggrieved at taking care of the baby but it looked to Emma as if he was having a great time.

Gracie and she were going to have to have a long talk. Soon.

"Dad?"

He turned to grin at her. "Hello, honey, what're you up to?"

"Oh, I was just…" She waved one hand toward the outside. "Straightening out the tack room."

He chuckled. "You always did have your mother's neat streak."

Emma walked up to him and sat down on the chair closest to him. "Gracie told me Buck quit."

He frowned. "He did, but couldn't blame him any. He's older than I am and damned if I'm out working the ranch every day."

The baby slapped both of her little hands on top of his and then played with his fingers.

"Got to remember to watch my language now, don't I?" He grinned down at Molly. "This little darling reminds me so much of you at her age."

Emma felt a tiny pang that she refused to identify or acknowledge. "Does she?"

"Always happy, always looking for the next thing…" His smile faded a bit, but his eyes were still shining. "I'm glad to have you home, Emma, and that's the truth."

She leaned forward, reached out and squeezed his hand briefly. "I'm glad somebody is." She blew out a breath in frustration. "Gracie sneers at me every time we pass by each other."

He laughed. "Well, Gracie's just put out. She's done her best these last five years, but she doesn't have your confidence. Never has. So she doubts everything she does."

Emma didn't like the sound of that. "Well, she shouldn't. She's always seemed so sure of herself to me. Even in school, she went her own way no matter what anyone else had to say."

"All true," he mused. "But at the heart of it, she questions herself."

"She hates me now." Emma picked at a fraying thread on the arm of the couch.

Frank laughed again. "No, she doesn't. She's just afraid to enjoy having you back. Probably thinking you're not going to stay."

Gracie wouldn't be worried about that in the slightest if she knew what had been a huge motivating factor in driving Emma home in the first place. Oh, she had been planning on coming back to Montana, but she'd pushed her schedule up fast for one reason only. But that wasn't something she could talk about. Not even with her family.

Watching her, Frank asked quietly, "Is she right? Are you just stopping by for a visit before you take off again?"

She couldn't blame her father for the question. When she left, Emma had had big plans. She'd done her best, and put everything she had into making those plans a reality. None of it had worked out and by the end of her time in California she had been wondering why she'd ever left Montana in the first place. Now she'd come home to build different dreams. And this time, she would succeed.

But it wasn't only her family and her home that had pulled her back to Montana. It was Caden. The cowboy she'd left behind. The man who could set her body ablaze with a look. The man who starred in her dreams nightly. The man she'd never been able to forget—not that she'd really tried.

"No, Dad," she said, leaning forward to lay her hand on his forearm. She wanted him to see her resolve. To feel that she was really back for good. Her gaze locked with his and she willed him to believe her. "Molly and I are home to stay."

He studied her for a long moment or two, then pleasure shone on his face. "Relieved to hear that, Em," he said. "Don't think I could stand watching you leave again and taking this little nugget with you."

"You don't have to worry," she assured him.

"And Molly's daddy?" Frank asked, sliding her a glance. "What's he have to say about all of this? Doesn't he mind you bringing his daughter to Montana?"

Emma went completely still, then forced her mouth to curve slightly. Molly's father wasn't someone she could talk about. This was dangerous territory. She hated lying to her own father, but there were some things she couldn't tell him. At least not now.

"Molly's father isn't involved with her at all, Dad. He doesn't know where we are and that's the way I hope it stays."

"Did he hurt you?" Instantly, her affable, loving dad went into grizzly mode.

Emma's heart swelled, relishing the feeling of being loved so fiercely. She actually didn't need protection, but it was lovely to have it offered so freely. And she was grateful that she could at least tell him the truth about this.

"No. He didn't." She got up, kissed his forehead and said, "Nothing like that. I swear."

"All right, then." He stroked one hand down Molly's silky black hair. "As long as you two are here and safe. That's all that's important."

"Just how I feel." And as long as Molly was safe, Emma could deal with just about anything. Then her father spoke up and tested that thought.

"Caden called me this morning."

Her gaze snapped to his. Warily, she asked, "What did he want?"

"Oh, just to tell me he was going to send some of his men over to mow the meadow behind the barn."

Frowning, Emma thought about that. Every year, they mowed the meadow, to protect it. The fallen grasses acted as mulch and the clipped-off seedpods planted themselves for the following spring. But since when did her ex take care of that?

"Why?" She straightened up and looked down at her father in disbelief. "First his men come and paint our fence. Now they're mowing our meadow?"

"Well," Frank mused, barely hiding the curve of his lips, "let's think about that. Could be, it's just him being neighborly. Could be, he's trying to impress you."

A choked-off laugh shot from her throat as she remembered clearly the look on his face when he'd murmured, *Absolutely nothing.* "No, it's not that, trust me."

"Seem awful sure."

"You didn't see him when he was here." She stalked over to the fireplace and idly noted that it had been turned into a gas hearth sometime while she was gone. Easier, probably. But she'd always loved the hiss and snap of real flames over real wood.

"No, but I saw him after you left for California."

She closed her eyes briefly, then looked back over her shoulder at her father. "I know I hurt him."

"Crushed him, more like."

Guilt reared up and took a bite of her heart. She knew her father was right. She'd known it then. It hadn't stopped her because she hadn't allowed it to. If she'd let herself acknowledge what she was doing to Caden—heck, to *herself*—by leaving, she might not have gone. And if she'd stayed, she'd still be wondering. Still be dreaming. Maybe Hollywood wasn't for her, but at least now, she knew that for herself. Still, she admitted silently, maybe she could have handled it better. "I had to go, Dad."

"I know that," Frank said, giving her an understanding smile. "Didn't make it any easier to lose you. I know why you had to leave, too. You think I didn't realize what your mother gave up to marry me and have our family?" He shook his head and sighed. "She had dreams, too, Emma, and she died not knowing if they could have come true. That still tears at me."

Emma instantly felt guilty for the pain she saw in her father's eyes. "Oh, Dad, Mom loved you. Loved us."

He snorted. "Hell, I know that. Doesn't mean a part of her wasn't wishing that she'd gone to Nashville and tried her hand at singing professionally." Frank smoothed the baby's hair and wistfully said, "That's why I was glad you tried, honey. As bad as it was with you gone, I was glad you were trying."

Tears stung her eyes and Emma blinked them back. At least her dad was glad to have her home. In the quiet, the baby cooed and gurgled in Frank's arms. Outside the windows, the October sky was leaden and a hard gust shook the turning leaves on the trees. A week ago, she'd been in Southern California, where the only sign of fall was the pumpkin spice lattes for sale on every corner. Here in Montana, the wind was cold, the trees golden and red and you could smell winter in the air.

It was good to be back. But, since she was here to stay, she would have to have a talk with Caden.

Absolutely nothing.

His voice repeated in Emma's mind again and she scowled to herself. Coming home was never going to be easy. She hadn't expected it to be. And she'd known that facing Caden again would be one of the hardest things she'd ever done, but she hadn't realized how hard it would be to not touch him. To not be touched by him. Seeing him again, hearing his voice had brought everything inside her back to life—only to be slapped down by his dismissal. She'd thought she was ready to see him again. Apparently, she'd been wrong.

"Things'll get better," her father said and she turned around to face him. He shifted the baby in his arms so that little Molly was looking directly at her. Emma's heart squeezed in her chest. That tiny girl had become all-important and there was simply nothing she wouldn't do to protect her. Bringing her here had assured that Molly would be cared for. Loved. It was up to Emma to see that she stayed that way.

"You'll find your path, and you brought my granddaughter home, too," Frank was saying and Emma's heart gave another hard lurch. "Your sister will get past what she's feeling. You two will work it out."

Emma wasn't so sure, but all right.

"As for me, though," Frank said, pushing up out of his chair and cradling Molly against his chest, "I couldn't be happier. Now I'm going to go give our girl here some lunch—"

"Dad," she said, remembering some of what Gracie had said just a while ago, "I didn't bring the baby here expecting you to babysit."

Insult stamped itself on his features. "Spending time with my granddaughter isn't 'babysitting,'" he told her. "Besides, makes me remember when my own girls were little. Your mother and I were hopping every minute."

A soft smile curved her mouth. "I still miss her."

"So do I, darling. Every damn day." Frank sighed a little, then grinned when Molly slapped her hands together. "She'd have loved this little one. So don't you worry about me and Molly. We're fine. You go and do something useful."

Something useful. Was talking to Caden a waste of time? Or a chance to set them both on a different path?

She watched her father walk away and thought about it. She could go back and finish cleaning out the tack room. Or she could go over the ranch books and see exactly where they stood financially. Or maybe go and talk to the cowboys and hear their opinions.

But she wasn't going to do any of that, Emma realized.

"Dad?"

He stopped and looked back at her, waiting.

Decision made, she said, "If it's okay with you, I'm going over to Caden's. Maybe settle a few things."

Her father winked. "That's a good idea, honey. You go ahead. Take your time."

When he left, Emma walked across the room and grabbed her heavy brown jacket off the coat tree in the hall. Take her time. That was assuming that Caden would speak to her at all. But even as she considered that, she remembered that she'd always been able to talk her way around that stubborn cowboy. Today would be no different.

They would get everything out in the open and find a way to deal with each other. Or, she considered, this would blow up in her face and she'd be no further along than she was right now.

Pulling her coat on, Emma stepped out onto the wide porch. There was a lot to do around here and she'd barely made a dent in any of it in the past few days.

But facing Caden was more important. All of the work would still be here waiting for her when she got back, she reminded herself. Digging her car keys out of her jacket pocket, she headed for the old and cranky SUV that had brought her and Molly all the way from Los Angeles.

She climbed in, fired it up and threw it into gear. Out by the stable, she saw Gracie talking to a woman with long, braided red hair and a face full of freckles. Must be the vet, she thought, then waved when Gracie turned to fire a glare at her. If her sister was mad, she only had herself to blame. She'd actually told Emma to stay away. So she would.

Turning the car around, she headed down the drive to the road that would take her to Caden's house. They were going to talk, damn it. And she wasn't going to take no for an answer.

Dirt and gravel flew up in her wake like the tail of a dragon and she barely noticed Gracie, standing in the yard, staring after her.

Three

Caden helped load the mare into a fancy horse trailer big enough for four horses. His buyer's teenage daughter was thrilled to be getting her own horse and he was pleased to have another satisfied customer.

Once the mare was inside and the back was closed, Caden walked to the front, opened the door and stepped inside. The mare tossed her pretty head when he entered and he had to smile.

"Yeah, you're a beauty and I'm sorry to lose you," he whispered, running his hands up and down her long, elegant neck. "But that girl out there is going to love you like crazy and spoil you even more than I do."

He stroked the star-shaped blaze on her forehead and just for a moment, allowed himself to remember the night this mare was born. Eight years ago. He and Emma had stayed up all night with Star's mother, talking, comforting, and they had been there when Star was born. Emma had been the one to name her and they'd planned to have Star be the first of a herd of beauties they would breed and build together.

Then they'd celebrated by making love in the loft above the stable.

God, he could still feel the heat, the magic of touching her, of being inside her, of having Emma's hands on his body.

Star whickered as if even the horse could judge his shift in mood. Well, hell, damned if he'd be so transparent an *animal* could read him. Shaking his head, Caden stroked her forehead one last time and said, "You be good to that girl and she'll love you all her life."

Just for a second, he thought about how ironic it was that he was selling Star now. Caden had thought that in letting the horse go, he'd be getting rid of the last real reminder of Emma on the ranch. Was it cosmic or karmic or just fate with a sense of humor to send Emma home now?

"It's a kick in the ass for damn sure," he muttered.

Then he turned his back on the past and walked out of the trailer and into an icy wind. Shaking hands with Matt Fraser, he said, "You've got a good horse there."

"We'll take care of her," the other man said.

Nodding, Caden looked at the man's daughter. About fourteen years old, she was practically vibrating with excitement.

"Your dad says you'll take good care of Star. Is that right?"

"I will," she said solemnly, her eyes locked on his face. "I promise I will."

He nodded. "If you do, that horse will love you forever."

"Thank you!" The words rushed from her and she impulsively gave Caden a hard hug. When she let him go, she looked up at him, eyes dazzled. "This is the best day of my whole life."

Caden smiled, despite the pang of regret he felt in losing Star. There was nothing quite like the relationship between a person and a horse.

And now, this young girl was clearly seeing a long, happy future ahead of her and Star. He hoped she had half the fun he'd had with River. "Well, you'd better get her home so you two can have a ride."

The girl raced to close the door on the trailer and jump into the front seat of her dad's truck. A few minutes later, the Frasers and Star were gone in a swirl of dust and wind.

Caden watched them go and realized that it was easier now to say goodbye. To let go. When Emma had left him, she'd ripped the earth out from beneath his feet. But she'd taught him something, too. He'd learned that he could survive loss.

And most importantly, he'd learned he couldn't trust Emma.

Gracie watched Emma drive off and a part of her wondered if she'd be back. She hated feeling the way she did, but Emma had hurt her deeply by leaving and that pain was still with her. How could she just forget? Forgive?

She huddled deeper into her jacket and pulled the collar up to protect her neck. Every winter, she thought about growing her hair out just because it would be warmer. Then in the summer, she was grateful it was short.

She tipped her head back to look at the sky and shivered a little at the gunmetal-gray clouds swarming in. Brightly colored leaves were ripped from the trees and sent tumbling on the icy afternoon wind.

"The place looks nice," Madison Peters said. "You got the corral fence painted."

Gracie smiled. "That was Caden. He sent some of his guys over to take care of it a couple days ago."

"He's a good friend," Madison mused.

"Yeah," Gracie said, "he is." Caden was someone she could always count on. He'd promised he'd take care of it and he had. When Caden gave his word, you could put money on it. That was something Gracie had really come to appreciate over the past five years. When she needed help, he was there. Unlike Emma.

Fresh anger erupted and bubbled in the pit of her stomach. She didn't like it. Didn't want to be so furious with the sister she'd loved so desperately most of her life. But how was she supposed to get past what she was feeling?

"Gracie, you've got to get over this thing with your sister."

She turned her head to look at the other woman, not even surprised that Madison had read what she was feeling. Her long red hair was pulled back in a braid, to keep it out of her way while she was working. Her pretty face was dotted with golden freckles and her green eyes shone like twin emeralds when she smiled. Which she wasn't doing at the moment.

"How'm I supposed to do that?"

Madison threw both hands up. "I don't know. Be grateful you have someone else here to help you with the ranch?" She tipped her head to one side and asked, "Aren't you always telling me that you need extra help here? Well, now Emma's home and you'll have it."

"Will I?" Gracie's mouth twisted. "She was in here straightening out the tack room earlier and now no one's going to be able to find anything."

Madison laughed. "I'm willing to thank her

for bringing a little order into that room. And you should, too."

"Now I should thank her?" Disgusted with Mad and with herself, Gracie turned her face into the wind. "No. She can't slide back into her own life like nothing ever happened."

"Is she really trying to do that?"

"Yeah," Gracie said, staring at the other woman. "She's acting like she never left! She's back in her old bedroom and she's taken over mom's sewing room for the baby…"

"You weren't using it for anything."

"You don't get it, Mad," Gracie said, shaking her head and pushing her own hair out of her eyes.

"Gracie…"

"She just does whatever the hell she feels like and screw what anyone else thinks about it."

Madison sighed. "You're just mad at her. Still."

"Of course I am."

Irritated that her friend wasn't able to understand what she was feeling, Gracie had to bite back a quick burst of anger. It wasn't surprising that she couldn't see this. Madison was new to Cache. She'd only moved there three years ago to take over the retiring vet's office. And almost from the moment they met, Mad and Gracie had been thick as thieves.

Taking a breath, Gracie now told herself to relax. Usually, she really appreciated Mad's optimistic, sunshiny attitude. But today, she'd really like her best friend to be on her side. "You weren't here when Emma left town. You don't know how hard it was. On everybody."

"You're right. I wasn't here," Madison agreed. "But you've told me about it. You've also told me how close you and Emma always were. So why're you so mad that she finally came home?"

"Whose side are you on?" Gracie asked, a little wounded that Madison was being so damn impartial.

The redhead laughed shortly. "Yours. I'm always on your side, Gracie. I just think maybe you should cut her a small break."

"Okay, what about this?" Gracie stepped in closer to Madison. "What if Emma's going to Caden's? What if he *tells* her?"

Worry flashed across Madison's eyes briefly and didn't do a thing to lessen Gracie's anxiety.

"Do you think he would?"

"No, but I didn't think Emma would ever come home, either, so don't go by my opinion."

"All right." Madison nodded sharply. "Let's say he *does* tell her. Would that really be so bad? Don't you have to tell her and your dad at some point?"

"Sure I do. But when I'm ready."

"And when will that be?" Madison's voice was small and Gracie winced.

"Soon. I swear, soon," she said and reached out to briefly squeeze Madison's hand.

"Secrets never stay secret, Gracie," Madison said.

"And I don't want it to," Gracie took a breath and chewed at her bottom lip. "Right now, I don't know how to tell them. But I'm going to figure it out. I swear."

"I know you will. And when you're ready, remember that I'm here for you." Madison gave her a smile. "But I'm not the only one who cares about you. You've got your dad. And now your sister. And the baby's here. You can't fool me, Gracie. I know how much you love kids. So let yourself love that baby."

Gracie sighed a little. She already did love that tiny girl, but she was afraid to let it show because what if Emma left? Again?

"How about," Madison continued, "when Emma comes home, you talk to her. Sit down, have a beer and just get it all out."

She laughed shortly. "Never thought I'd say this, but a beer can't solve everything."

"It's a start..."

"Why do you have to be so understanding all the time?"

"Because someone has to be." Madison asked, "Are you mad she left? Or mad she came home?"

"Both." Gracie waved one hand before Madison could say anything. "And yes, I know that makes zero sense."

Madison grinned. "Well, at least you know it."

Scowling, Gracie looked at the other woman. "You're not helping."

"I don't know how to help." She shrugged, and grabbed her bag before heading into the stable. Gracie stuck with her and Madison kept talking. "You and Emma used to be close."

"Key words there being *used to be*."

They walked into the stable and Madison headed for the far stall, where Diamond, an aging stallion, was waiting. "Uh-huh, but she's back. And the only thing stopping the two of you from being close again, is *you*."

"It's not the only thing," Gracie muttered darkly. She was feeling like a temperamental child throwing a tantrum. And speaking of child… "And she's got a baby she never bothered to tell us about. Who does that, Mad? Who doesn't tell her family that she's pregnant?"

Madison glanced at her before stepping into the stall. "We all have secrets, don't we, Gracie?"

She flushed and didn't like it. "Okay, good point. But she's clearly expecting Dad and I to take care of Molly."

"You love kids." Madison cooed and soothed the horse, then slowly bent to inspect the small nick on his foreleg.

"Not the point."

"What *is* the point, Gracie?"

Irritated, frustrated and just feeling so not herself, Gracie snapped, "The point is, Queen Emma has arrived and all of us peasants are expected to toss confetti her way."

Madison straightened up, looked at her for a long second or two, then burst out laughing. "Honestly, you're really going over the top here, Gracie. She's your sister. She came home. Sure, you can be upset, but she's *family*. That hasn't changed."

Gracie stuffed both hands into her jacket pockets and faced her friend. "I can't forget that she left."

"No one's asking you to," Madison said, bent down again, to medicate and wrap the small cut on the horse's leg. When she was finished, she stood up, and looked at Gracie across the half-door of the stall. "All I'm saying is that maybe you set the last five years aside—" she held up one hand when Gracie would have spoken "—and try to find your way from here."

"I don't know…" Gracie turned her head to look toward the open double doors and the darkening day outside. "She wasn't here, Mad. When I really needed her, she wasn't here."

Sighing a little, Madison left the stall, and set her bag down. Then she hugged Gracie tightly before taking a step back and meeting her eyes. "I know, honey. And it was hard for you. But you got through. And maybe it was a good thing that you had to face things on your own. Make the hard decisions and learn what you really wanted."

Giving her a wry smile, Gracie said, "Have I told you that I really hate it when you're so rational?"

"That's why I do it," Mad told her with a quick grin.

Gracie gave her a hard hug, then let her go. "Fine. I'll try." She narrowed her eyes. "I make no promises, but I'll try."

"That's good enough," Madison said. "Now, Diamond should be fine, but I'll be back tomorrow to check on him."

"That's the best news I've had today. I like when you're here."

"I'm glad," Madison said with a quick, impish grin. "Now, why don't you walk me out to my truck?"

"Sure." Gracie fell into step beside her. "Are we still on for dinner tonight?"

"As long as the Callahan's cow doesn't go into labor," Madison said. "Fingers crossed. I'll call you if I can't make it. Otherwise, I'll meet you at the Little River Diner at five."

Gracie opened the door and held it while Madison climbed in. "Thanks for listening to me rant."

Madison grinned again and her bright green eyes sparkled. "Not a problem. Now you owe me the next time I need to vent."

"Deal."

She patted Gracie's hand. "Don't be so hard on Emma. She might surprise you."

"Yeah. That's what I'm afraid of," Gracie admitted.

* * *

On the short ride to Caden's Emma rehearsed what she wanted to say. Not that it would help. The minute she saw him again, her mouth would go dry and her heart would hammer in her chest. Caden had been having that effect on her for as long as she could remember.

And during the years she was in California, surrounded by men who were deliberately gorgeous and continually posing to put themselves in the best possible light, she hadn't met a single one as amazing as the cowboy she'd left behind.

"This is such a bad idea," she told herself sternly, driving along the narrow road.

Seeing him, being with him, was only going to stir up more of the feelings he'd made it clear he wasn't interested in reviving. But she was home now. She wasn't leaving again. Caden's ranch was so close to hers and Cache was such a small town, they'd be seeing each other all the time. So they had to find a way to be together without a constant state of war between them. "That would just be exhausting."

She glanced into the rearview mirror and wished she'd taken the time to put on some eye makeup or something. But if she'd waited, she might have avoided facing Caden at all. So she was going to face down her former lover without a shred of makeup and with her hair in a tangle from the wild, cold wind rushing across Montana.

She gave her reflection a quick glare. "Why do you care what you look like? It's not as if you're going over there to seduce him."

Though that thought set up a flicker of fire that had her shifting uncomfortably in her seat. A moment later, her mind lit up with memories. God, sex with Caden had spoiled her for any other man. Not that she'd lived like a vestal virgin for the five years she was gone. But no one had come close to making her feel what Caden could with a single touch.

Images raced through her mind, one after another. Moonlit nights in Caden's arms. The two of them, naked and wrapped around each other in a sunlit meadow. Sex in a canoe that had ended up being sex in the lake once they'd capsized the narrow boat. Her lips twisted into a reluctant smile, but in the next instant, that smile faded.

Everything was different now.

Familiar countryside stretched out on either side of the road. Trees, meadows, the last lingering wildflowers, already bent in half by the cold wind bringing winter. So much was the same, and yet so much had changed.

Caden had once been not only her lover, but her best friend. The one person she could go to with anything. He had been her touchstone.

Now he was a stranger to her and seemingly way too close to her little sister. Gracie had gone running over to Caden's three times in the few days Emma had been home. Why? What was going on there?

She remembered how Gracie had thrown herself into Caden's arms two days ago. She'd also heard her sister on the phone with him several times since then and late last night, Gracie had gone to Caden's place again to "talk." Anger bubbled inside and with it, some jealousy, as well. Was Gracie going after Caden because he'd once been Emma's? Was Caden doing the same thing?

She chewed at her bottom lip and ignored the swarms of what felt like dragons in the pit of her stomach.

Her hands tightened on the steering wheel. "If he's using Gracie to get back at me, that's going to stop today."

She made the turn into the Double H drive and familiarity stirred inside. How many times had she come down this road, to this ranch, running to Caden? She couldn't even count them all.

And Emma remembered that she and Caden had once planned to lay out a road linking their two ranches. Going straight across their land, it would be a private road, cutting ten minutes off the trip, making sure their families could always reach each other in a hurry.

But that plan had died along with so many others when she'd left Montana. Oaks, elms and aspen trees lined the drive and the fall jewel tones of gold and red and orange were bright splashes of color in a gray day. The wind drove fallen leaves into mini-tornadoes that drifted across the front of her SUV and temporarily blinded her.

Once they'd passed, Emma spotted the ranch house and came to a dead stop.

This was not the house she remembered. Five years ago, Caden's place had been big, but not pala-tial. *This* house was a Western palace.

Two stories, with a steep roof for the snow to slide off, the front was a wall of glass that would provide a spectacular view of Flathead Lake. River stone and golden oak planks made up the walls and lined the wide balcony off the first floor where several chairs were gathered around what she assumed was a gas firepit. The front porch was flanked by black iron sconces and the surrounding trees stood like soldiers on guard duty.

Simply staggered by the beauty of it all, Emma wondered what had happened while she was gone to allow Caden to build this place.

After a second or two, she continued on and noted the much bigger barn and an even larger stable with a corral that seemed to take up almost an acre of land. Caden had done just what he'd always planned to do. Taken his father's ranch and expanded it, made it something extraordinary. Of course, the plan was always that Emma would be a part of it. They'd both had dreams for this place and something tugged at her insides when she had to admit that he'd done it all without her.

She parked the SUV outside the house and got out, hunching deeper into her jacket. The wind was more fierce now and the icy chill was slicing into her bones. It had been a long time since she'd faced a Montana fall and winter, but she'd been raised here and so she knew that the weather could turn on you in a heartbeat. She glanced up at the leaden sky and told herself it would probably be best not to stay long. Of course, that might not be an issue. Caden might not be here. And if he was, he could refuse to talk to her.

"Emma, is that you?"

She looked up and smiled, grateful for the reprieve from her thoughts. "Hi, Jack. Good to see you."

Jack Franklin. Caden's best friend and foreman. Of course, once upon a time, Jack and his wife, Gwen, had been *her* friends, too. Now she wasn't so sure. "Is Caden around?"

"Yeah." He frowned a little, tugged the brim of his hat down on his forehead and glanced over his shoulder at the stable. "He's with one of our pregnant mares."

Her gaze drifted to the stables as well, as if she could see through the dark green wood walls to the man inside. "Everything all right?"

"Oh, sure," Jack said. "You know Caden, though. He takes care of what's his."

She shifted her gaze to the man and wondered if he was trying for some subtext. But he looked innocent enough. Hard to tell, though. Jack's loyalty would be to his friend. "I saw Gwen at the grocery store the other day."

"Yeah, she told me." He smiled at her and shook his head. "Feels weird, having you back. But good, at the same time. It's hard, isn't it?"

"Really is," she agreed, taking a little hope from Jack's attitude. "Look, I'm home to stay, Jack. I know Caden's not happy with me…"

He snorted.

She winced. "I just want to make things right, you know?"

"I get it Emma." His smile faded, but his eyes were still kind. "But it's not going to be easy."

She shrugged and said, "When was talking to Caden about something he didn't want to, *ever* easy?"

He nodded. "Good point. Okay, tell you what. Why don't you go on in the house? I'll let Caden know you're here."

She glanced at the big, beautiful building behind her, then back to Jack. "Okay, I will. Thanks."

"Not a problem." He turned to go and stopped when she spoke up again.

"Jack? Say hi to Gwen for me."

He grinned. "I will. And if it helps…she's really glad you're home again."

"It does. Thanks." She didn't watch him go. Instead, Emma walked up the steps to the wide front door and silently admired the carving of pines dug deeply into the wood. Entering the house, she had to stop again to admire it all. The floors were wide planked oak, with colorful rugs tossed here and there to break up the starkness. The great room held brown leather couches and chairs, heavy, wide tables and a few lamps that would spill golden light across the entire room when turned on.

The fireplace was river stone, with a thick slab of carved oak as a mantel. On the mantel was a windup clock she remembered Caden's mother had bought on a trip to Germany one year and on either side of that, were silver candlestick holders that had been in Caden's father's family for generations. The painting over the hearth was of the original ranch house and only served to bring home how much the Hale ranch had changed over the last few years.

The view of the lake was spectacular, that wall of windows displaying the amazing landscape like an oversize painting. But she turned from that view and walked toward the French doors on the far wall that opened onto the balcony. Inside the beautiful house, it was warm and luxurious and downright cozy, but Emma couldn't take it. The unfamiliarity of the place. The knowledge that Caden had done all of this without her. That he'd done so well on his own while her adventure in dream chasing had ended with a mind-numbing thud.

Shaking her head, she pushed through one of the doors into the icy wind that slapped at her and somehow felt more welcoming than the warmth of the house. Her boots sounded softly against the deck as she walked to the railing and watched the ranch at work. Cowboys were in the corral, working several horses. She could smell a fire and noted smoke lifting out of the chimney of what she guessed was Jack and Gwen's house.

And then he stepped out of the stable, a tall, muscled cowboy and all Emma could think was *Caden*.

Four

Caden stopped dead and looked across the yard to the house. To *her*.

Ridiculous to even think it, but Emma could have sworn he was looking directly into her eyes. She felt the solid punch of his stare even from a distance and knew that she still wanted him. More than anything else in her life, she wanted his hands on her. His mouth on hers. Remembering the fire that rose up between them made her hunger for that heat.

In spite of everything—or hell, maybe *because* of everything that had happened to her since she'd been gone, that need for Caden was as sharp as ever.

He was headed her way, a tall man, with broad shoulders, narrow hips and long legs. His black hair hung over the collar of his jacket and gave him a piratical look that did absolutely wicked things to Emma. But then, looking at Caden had always made her want…too much.

He kept his gaze fixed on her as he strode across the yard and as he came closer, her heartbeat quickened and her mouth went dry. *Seriously?* She'd come here furious that he might be using her sister. She'd come here hurt that he was so willing to have nothing to do with her. She'd arrived ready to have it out with him—and now all she wanted was to *have* him.

Coming here might not have been such a good idea.

She turned, went inside and was standing beside the cold hearth when he walked into the room. How one cowboy could completely take over a huge space simply by standing there was a question for the ages. But the simple truth was, Caden could.

"What're you doing here, Emma?"

Good question. Watching him now, so close, yet so far away, tore at her and made Emma want all kinds of things from this moment. She wanted to rewind time and have the years separating them simply disapper. Yet, at the same time, she couldn't wish it away and instead she wanted him to accept what she'd done. And mostly, she wanted him to want her.

None of that was happening at the moment, though, so she gave herself a mental kick and said, "We have to talk, Caden."

"No, we really don't." He took his hat off and sailed it like a tan Frisbee to the nearest couch. Shrugging out of his green jacket, he dropped that on a chair and stalked to the bar across the room.

"Caden—"

"I mean it," he said, tossing a quick look at her. "We don't have anything to talk about, Em."

Em. He used to call her that and stupidly, she took heart from the use of that casual nickname now. There was nothing on his gorgeous face that should encourage her and yet…apparently *hope* was a hard kill.

She took her jacket off too and dropped it onto a chair before walking over to him. He grabbed a beer from the bar fridge, opened it and took a long drink. No friendly offer of one for her, so Emma didn't wait. She got one for herself and ignored his raised eyebrow. After a sip of beer, she looked up at him. "I want to know what's going on between you and Gracie."

"And I want you to go home," he said flatly. "Guess we're both going to be disappointed."

Turning his back on her, he headed to the fireplace and hit a switch tucked away behind one of the river stones used to frame it. Gas flames shot up instantly and danced along faux logs.

Surprised, she said, "You always liked real fireplaces better."

He shot her a look. "Things change."

That was plain enough.

Caden shook his head, took another drink of his beer and shrugged. "It's both. I can change it to a wood burner when I want to."

Was that a concession? Really? Was that how sad she was now? Taking a casual statement about a fireplace as a sign that maybe he didn't hate her? She looked into his eyes and felt flames lick at her insides. Didn't seem to matter that he hadn't welcomed her with open arms.

Caden was dynamite to her match.

He turned away and studied the dancing flames in a taut silence that scraped at her raw nerves.

Cradling her beer between her hands, she welcomed the cold and silently hoped it would ease the heat engulfing her. Emma glanced at the glass French doors separating them from the outside world and reminded herself that every cowboy on this ranch could look through that glass and see whatever happened in this room. Not that anything *was* happening.

She dropped onto one of the leather couches to watch him. It took a few more minutes of strained silence, but finally, he turned to look down at her. "You're not leaving, are you?"

Emma shook her head. "Not until we talk."

Both of his eyebrows shot up. "Hope you brought some luggage with you, because that's going to be a while."

Irritation had her blurting, "Caden, you can't just ignore me."

"Why the hell not? Just what you did to me for five years."

Guilt pinged inside her, but she squashed it. No, she hadn't written to him or called, but she'd done that deliberately at first. Moving away from him, from Montana, hadn't been easy and she'd convinced herself that talking to Caden or clinging to the memory of him would only make the move that much harder. And then she'd found work and lost it and found something else and got in trouble and she hadn't wanted to talk to him. To tell him that she'd made a mistake by going to California. That she'd failed. Because what would have been the point?

"I left because I had to," she said quietly.

"Yeah, I remember the speech, thanks." He took another drink of his beer.

"But I'm back now."

"And what do you expect me to do? Handsprings?"

"And did you expect me to stay away?"

"Why wouldn't I?" he demanded and slammed his beer bottle down on the mantel hard enough to rattle the silver candlesticks. "You walked out on everything, Emma. Why should I think you'd come back? And now that we're down to it, why *did* you come back? Hollywood not living up to your expectations?"

Not even close, she thought but didn't say.

"I had to bring Molly home," she said instead.

He shook his head, then pushed both hands through his hair. God, just watching his muscles shift and move beneath his white long-sleeved shirt was earth-shattering. Her fingers actually itched to rip his shirt open and slide her hands across that muscled chest. To feel his heartbeat. To watch fire explode in his eyes.

"That's right," he said with a snort. "You came home with a *baby*. Who's the lucky father, Emma? Where the hell is he? Did he walk out on you like you walked out on me? Or did you leave him, too?"

Emma stiffened, then forced herself to relax so he wouldn't see. Wouldn't notice her reaction to the mention of Molly's father. She wouldn't talk about the baby. Not now.

Instead, she picked up on the last thing he'd said and argued the point. "Damn it, Caden, I didn't just walk out." Ready to defend herself, she stood up and faced him. "I talked to you about it. I *told* you that I had to do this. Hell, I asked you to go to California *with* me. Or did you forget that part?"

"I remember. Everything," he added, meeting her gaze with a cold stare that sent shivers along her spine. "You asked me to go with you but you knew I couldn't."

"Couldn't?" she argued. "Or *wouldn't*?"

"Both." He kept his eyes locked with hers and

when he spoke again, his voice was so deep, so soft, it seemed to vibrate inside her, plucking every nerve.

"I had to be here, Emma," he said. "And you knew that. My life is here. This ranch. Building it into something special. That was my dream. Used to be yours, too. Or did you forget how many nights we spent planning what we'd build here?"

"I remember. Everything." She used his own words to make her point. "And you're right, Caden. It was my dream, too," she said quietly, owing him that much. To let him know she hadn't been pretending all those nights when the two of them would talk and plan and dream. "It was just that—"

"Other dreams came first?"

"Why don't you understand why I had to try?" She'd come here wanting to have it out with him, but it seemed they were just talking in circles, not solving anything, just dredging up more misery.

"I didn't want to understand, Emma. All I needed to know was, you left."

"And how long are you going to be throwing that in my face?"

"How long you going to be here?"

A verbal slap that set her back a step or two. She didn't remember him being this shut down. This cold. Or hard. Was she supposed to take the blame for that, as well?

"This was a mistake. So fine. I'll go." She grabbed her coat.

"Leaving must get easier the more you do it," he mused, still with that quiet, cold tone.

"Damn it, Caden," she argued, tossing her hair back behind her shoulders. "You just *told* me to go."

"Don't."

She dropped her coat again and stared at him. "Why?"

He crossed his arms over his broad chest and stood tall and gorgeous, staring at her. "You came here to talk, right?"

"Yeah."

"Then let's talk."

"Quick turnaround," she mused, wondering why he was being so reasonable all of a sudden.

"Living in Hollywood cause you to be this suspicious?" he asked.

Yes. "No," she said, tipping her head to one side to study him. "I just know you, Caden, and—"

He cut her off neatly. "You used to know me, Emma. Things change."

Pain tugged at her heart. "Yeah, I've noticed."

His jaw clenched and the muscle there twitched. "Come on back to the kitchen. I'm hungry and if we're going to have one of our 'conversations,' I'm gonna need my strength."

He headed out of the room and Emma followed him. True, they used to have some wonderful arguments back in the day. They were both stubborn and unwilling to admit when they were wrong, so those fights could go on for hours. And back then, they'd usually ended one of their *talks*, in bed—or on the ground, against a wall, in a hay loft...

The thought of that happening today sent a jolt of anticipation through her. She wondered if he was remembering. Wondered if he was wanting as badly as she was. Maybe he was right about needing strength.

As she walked behind him, Emma tried to keep her gaze off of his butt, so she distracted herself by looking at the rest of his amazing house. A long hallway led past a dining room with a hand-carved table big enough to seat twenty. There were paintings on the wall, depicting different sections of the ranch, the town of Cache and the river that cut through Caden's property and led up to the mountains. It was a showplace. Everything he'd ever dreamed of building and more.

Then she followed him into the kitchen and just stopped in the doorway to admire it.

For the past five years, she'd been sharing a tiny two-bedroom apartment in West Hollywood with her roommate, Terry. Their kitchen counter had been the size of a breadboard with a sink barely big enough to set a plate down into it. In fact, you could have fit the entire apartment in Caden's kitchen.

The cupboards were a pale oak with copper pulls. There was open shelving on the walls as well, where pitchers, platters and coffee mugs were stored. A huge island in the center of the room was topped with a slab of dark brown and white granite so huge that it must have taken ten men to carry in and install. An immense, hammered copper range hood over the eight-burner stove and an oversize refrigerator also covered in that same burnished copper.

Eight stools were pulled up to the island and a window over the sink that was wide enough to provide a glorious view of the lake. At one end of the room, there was a big round table with six chairs sitting in front of another window, this one with a view of the ranch yard and the pines that stood guard behind the buildings.

"This is…" she said on a breathy sigh, *"perfect."*

He glanced at her and she saw the flash of pride in his eyes before he buried it. "Yeah, had this place built a few years ago. Figured to make the kitchen as big as possible, since we sometimes end up with all the hands in here, looking for a hot meal."

A few years ago. How had he done all of this so quickly? The old ranch house had been small and cozy, the place where Caden had grown up, and now it had been displaced by a mansion that was simply breathtaking.

He tossed her a quick look as he opened the fridge and pulled out a covered plate of sandwiches.

Her eyes went wide. "Wow, the refrigerator is magic, too? You're hungry and it provides ready-made food?"

One corner of his mouth twitched. "No, this is courtesy of my housekeeper."

She'd guessed that of course. "Does she live here?" Emma really hoped not. If they were going to be able to really argue and get everything between them out in the open—then she didn't want to have to worry about someone overhearing them.

"No," he said, setting the plate onto the island and reaching back into the fridge for a beer. He held it up. "Do you want one?"

"Sure." She grabbed a couple of paper towels, then took a seat on one of the island stools. "So she drives in from Cache every day? That's got to be challenging in winter." When that long, two-lane road became so packed with snow it could sometimes take *days* for the county to plow it.

He took a seat opposite her, twisted off the caps on the beer bottles and handed one to her. "No, Victoria lives on the ranch. Her husband, Micah Taylor, is the barn boss."

She nodded, understanding. A barn boss took care of the hiring and firing of people, though he'd work with the foreman on making those decisions. Plus he ran the schedules, ordered feed and made sure work was getting done.

The foreman oversaw *everything*. The men, the horses, the ranch itself. They also used both recognized and innovative breeding practices to improve the animal stock. Plus the foreman was in charge of the employees, and maintaining the ranch itself.

She handed Caden one of the paper towels as he peeled the plastic wrap off the plate. "Help yourself. Looks like there's ham and turkey today."

"Your favorite," she mused, and took a half a sandwich.

One eyebrow lifted. "You remember."

It wasn't a question. "We've known each other most of our lives," she pointed out. "Hard to not know."

"Uh-huh." He took a bite of his sandwich and while he chewed, he studied her.

Emma just barely managed to not shift positions beneath that steady stare. Fire was licking at her bloodstream and her heartbeat was accelerating with every breath she drew. Her skin felt electric, as if her body was pumping out a low-level buzz. Her gaze drifted from his eyes to his mouth, his strong jaw and then his Adam's apple as he swallowed, then took a swig of beer.

What was it about this man? How could she be reacting *exactly* as she had when she'd walked away from him all those years ago? Shouldn't this feeling have gotten fainter? Instead, it was as if her body had only been waiting for her to get close to him again to remind her just what she was capable of.

"You're staring," he said.

"You started it," she countered and lifted her gaze to his again.

She wished she could read his eyes as easily as she used to be able to. But apparently, he'd gotten better at hiding what he was thinking because all she saw in those lake-blue depths was a deliberate distance—and the hint of a smoldering fire. God, she'd missed that fire.

Setting his beer down onto the granite with a soft click, he said, "You wanted to talk, Emma."

"Yeah, I do." But where to start? Trying to explain *again* why she'd left Montana—and him? Demanding an explanation of what was going on between him and her sister? Even as she considered it, she realized that *demanding* was never the way to go with Caden. Any more than it was with her. Should she ask how he'd managed to build his dream ranch in the same amount of time that she was in California seeing her dreams die?

He was watching her. Waiting. And before she could stop herself, Emma blurted something she hadn't planned to say. "I missed you, Caden."

He looked surprised, though why he should have been, she couldn't have said.

"You didn't *have* to miss me, Emma."

"Maybe I did," she said. "Maybe I had to find out what was really important to me before I could appreciate what I had."

Wow. Was that true? It felt true. Being in Hollywood, surrounded by strangers, at first, she'd avoided thinking of him, of this place, her family, so she wouldn't miss them all so deeply. But as time passed, she'd dredged up memories of Caden, and her home and family, to keep her sane.

He shook his head, stood up and stalked a few paces away from her as if he couldn't sit still another minute. "You're not really going to try to convince me that you leaving was a *good* thing."

"No." He'd never believe it, but Emma did. She'd discovered a lot of truths about herself while she was gone. She'd learned that she wasn't cut out to live in the fast lane no matter what her dreams had been. The mountains and lakes and rivers were where she belonged. She'd learned what was important and what she could toss aside.

Most important, she'd realized that Caden was still at the heart of what she wanted. Needed. But why would he believe that?

"Caden, the important thing is I'm back now. And I'm not going anywhere."

He shoved one hand through his hair with an impatient gesture. "And I should take your word for that."

"You don't have to." She stood up, too, and walked toward him, stopping just out of reach. "You'll see it. I'll be right there at the ranch. I'll be in town. At the diner. In church. We'll be seeing a lot of each other whether you like it or not, so you're going to have to find a way to deal with it. With *me*."

"Think so, do you?"

"Well, what else?" she snapped, throwing both hands high. "Are you going to actively ignore me? Come and go from my family's ranch and not look at me? Play house with my sister and not give me a thought?"

His eyes narrowed. "I told you what's between me and Gracie is none of your business."

"You're wrong about that," Emma argued, feeling her temper spike along with her lust. "Gracie's my business and you used to be—"

"Key words there being *used to be*."

"Right. Fine. But damned if I'll watch you go from me to Gracie."

"Oh?" One dark eyebrow lifted and he gave her a sardonic smile. "Who put you in charge of who I sleep with?"

She sucked in a gulp of air. "So you're admitting it? You're having sex with my *sister*?"

"My sex life is none of your damn business, Emma. How many times do I have to say it?"

Emma was appalled. And yet…he hadn't really said he was, had he? Was he screwing with her just to make her crazier? That completely sounded like Caden. And really, as pissed as Gracie had been for days, if she was having sex with Emma's old boyfriend, she would have thrown the fact in Emma's face long before now.

Okay, maybe she was overreacting here.

"Were you celibate in California?" he taunted, taking a step to close the distance between them. "No guys coming to your bed? No Hollywood pretty men getting you naked and on your back?"

Did the thought of her with other men bother him? Sure seemed to. That was a good sign, wasn't it? If he didn't care, he wouldn't give a damn who she'd been with.

"I never said I was celibate and you weren't, either—" She didn't know that for sure, of course, but she couldn't imagine that Caden had stayed faithful to the memory of a woman who had walked out on him. Though damn it, she hated the images floating in her mind.

Of Caden's muscled, strong body covering some other woman, burying himself inside her, driving her to the brink of insanity as he'd once done to her. She *hated* that. Especially if that woman was Gracie.

"Damn straight I wasn't," he ground out and moved even closer, looking down at her, forcing her to look up to meet his eyes. "When you left, I lost myself in so many women I damn near couldn't keep track of them all."

She swallowed a knot of bitterness clogging her throat, but even at that, she realized that he hadn't had just *one* woman who had meant something to him. "You needed dozens of women to take *my* place, did you?"

"Yes." He snapped the word and he didn't look happy about the admission. "Like knowing that? Like knowing that you left such a gaping hole inside me that the more I tried to fill it, the emptier I felt?"

"Of course not," she whispered, caught by his gaze. There were fires there now, not smoldering, but hot, licking flames that swept over her skin, igniting every nerve ending until she felt as if she was bristling with sexual need.

"I was empty, too, Caden."

"By choice, Emma."

True again. She swallowed hard, and reached for him, half-afraid that he'd step away from her, leaving her shattered just to teach her a lesson. But he didn't move. If anything, he went completely still.

She hadn't come here for this, at least not consciously. But maybe this was what had been driving her since she got home. The need to touch him and be touched. To remember what it felt like to be so alive that she practically glowed. She wanted him more than she ever had before and if he pushed her away, the pain of it might kill her.

Emma moved up to him and kept her gaze locked with his. Laying both hands on his shoulders, she looked into his lake-blue eyes and said, "We've been empty too long, Caden. Fill me up. Fill us both."

"Damn you for leaving, Emma." His gaze moved

over her face, then met her eyes. "And damn you for coming back."

Then he grabbed her, pulled her in close and bent his head to hers. His eyes locked with hers, his heated stare seemed to burn right through her. "This could be a mistake. For both of us. Are you sure you want to do this?"

"More sure than I've ever been about anything in my life," she told him breathlessly.

"Me, too," he admitted. "Damn it."

Five years fell away and once again it was just the two of them, combustible, eagerly leaping into the flames. Emma looked up into his eyes and saw hunger there. That need was something she'd always responded to. Now was no different.

She went up on her toes and took his mouth with hers. For one brief, shining moment, there were fireworks inside. And God how she'd missed them. Then he broke that kiss, pulled away and she was left staring at him, breathing hard.

"What're you doing?"

He walked to the wall, hit a switch and glanced back at her. "Damned if I'm putting on a show for the cowboys out there."

"What?" Confusion clouded her mind even more than the desire swirling through her.

"The windows," he said, coming back to her. "Got a lot of them."

"I noticed."

"Well, that switch I just threw darkens the glass so no one sees in."

Truth be told she hadn't given the walls of glass in this palace a single thought. She would have jumped him right here and never realized that the whole world could be watching—and maybe she wouldn't have cared. As long as she had his hands on her again.

"Good thinking." Then she stopped talking when he kissed her again, taking her mouth with a frenzied need that fired up everything she was already feeling. His hunger was as sharp and insistent as hers.

His tongue parted her lips, swept into her mouth and made her knees weak. Emma actually slumped against him and Caden pulled her in close and tight, his arms coming around her like steel bands.

He tasted her over and over again, never giving her a chance to catch her breath. And Emma didn't care. Breathing didn't matter. Nothing mattered but this moment. *Him.* His hands swept up and down her spine, then down to her butt so he could pull her hard against him. So she would feel his erection pressing into her. So she would want him even more than she did already. And just when she was ready to tear both of their clothes off and stretch out on the kitchen floor, Caden broke the kiss again.

"Are you doing that on purpose?" she asked as she swayed unsteadily.

"What?"

"Kissing me senseless then abruptly stopping. Because if you're doing it to make me crazy, you should know…it's working." She tossed her hair back from her face and looked up at him in time to see a flash of humor that quickened and died in his eyes in a heartbeat.

"No," he assured her, hooking one arm around her waist and leading her out of the room. He kept her pressed tightly to his side as he said, "But damned if we're doing this on the floor."

"It's a nice floor," she argued.

"Not as nice as my bed."

Five

Emma's stomach fluttered and her pulse jumped into a jackhammer beat. He led her down the hall, and she hurried to keep up with his long-legged stride. The main staircase loomed up in the foyer, with hand-turned spindles and a carved oak banister that made it look like one long branch sprouting thousands of leaves. There was a dark red runner in the middle of the stairs that muffled their steps and as they moved, Emma glanced at the windows and saw that they'd all darkened at the flip of the switch Caden had turned on.

"Everyone out there will guess what we're doing, won't they?" she wondered aloud, still hurrying alongside him.

He shrugged, kept her close and stepped up his pace. "Do you care?"

"Not a bit."

"Good." At the top of the staircase, he turned right, headed for the door at the end of the hall.

Pulling her into his bedroom, Caden kicked the door closed behind them and Emma took a quick look around. The wall facing the lake was glass here as well, but it too was dark, muting the already weak October sunlight until it was barely noticeable. The pines surrounding the lake were bending with the wind, the gray, stormy skies had lowered threateningly and the lake itself looked like a sheet of molten silver.

She barely had time to notice the stone fireplace on one wall, the chests and dressers against two other walls and the massive bed that was clearly the centerpiece of the room. Here, too, he'd had someone carve a head- and footboard with scenes of the lake, the pines and the horses Caden raised and trained. The bed itself was gigantic and covered in a forest green comforter accompanied by what looked like dozens of pillows.

Then his hands were on her and she couldn't have cared less about the furniture.

"After five years without you, this is gonna be fast, Emma," he warned, cupping her breasts, and all she could think about was she wanted her clothes gone so she could feel his skin against hers.

"Nothing wrong with fast," she assured him and tore at her clothes. He did the same and in just a few seconds, they were naked, wrapped together and tumbling back onto the big bed. His body was hot, muscled and strong. He was hard and ready and she didn't want to waste another minute, so Emma rolled with him until she was straddling him, then went up on her knees.

Smiling, she would have taken him inside her in the next instant, but his big hands settled at her waist, lifted her and tossed her to one side.

Emma slapped one hand down on the bed. "Damn it, Caden, stop stopping!"

"You always were too bossy for your own good," he muttered and reached out to the bedside table. He yanked the top drawer open, pulled out a condom and ripped the foil packet open.

Emma blew out a breath. God, she was an idiot. Running on hormones and want, she'd have had unprotected sex just to feel him inside her again. "I hate when you're right."

He glanced at her and grinned. "Well, then, I guess some things *don't* change."

"Funny." She went up on her elbows, cocked her head to one side and asked, "Ready now?"

"You gonna argue our way through this, like old times?"

"I will if you don't get inside me in the next ten seconds."

"Like I said, bossy," Caden rasped, then grabbed her, pulled her close and spread her thighs. "Always liked that about you."

His fingers smoothed up and down her heated, damp core and with every caress, Emma squirmed, shifted, even whimpered a little. Planting her feet on the mattress, she rocked her hips to the rhythm of his touch and felt that hidden, coiled spring inside her tighten further.

"You're still not inside me," she ground out.

"You're still not the boss of me," he told her, then scooped his hands beneath her butt and lifted her off the mattress.

"Caden!" Emma's eyes glazed over as his mouth closed over her center. His tongue stroked her, dipped inside and then stroked again. His lips and teeth nibbled at her and when he tasted that one hard, hot nub of sensation, Emma nearly flew off the mattress.

Helpless, her hips rocked spasmodically as he took her, forcing her to feel, to accept, to give herself up to what he could do to her body. It had always been like this between them, a small part of Emma's brain acknowledged. No matter what, Caden touched her and it was magic. She'd never found this with anyone else. It was him. Only Caden could break through her own sense of self to make her admit that they were more together than they were apart.

That had scared her five years ago.

Now, she just wanted more.

When the first ripples of release hit her, she screamed his name, gripped her fingers into the comforter and held on as her world rocked around her. And before her body had stopped trembling, Caden was there, pushing himself into her depths, claiming her in the most intimate way possible.

She gasped at that first invasion. He was so big, she could feel her body stretching to accommodate him and the marvelous friction he created when he moved within her, stoked the fire between them.

Emma moved with him, locked her legs around his hips and drew him higher, deeper, wanting all of him. Wanting him to be such a part of her that she wouldn't be able to let him go again.

His hips pistoned against her in a fierce rhythm that stole her breath even while it encouraged her to match his frantic moves. Emma did, racing toward completion, loving the feel of him, reeling in the memories and the now, tangling together in her mind and heart and body. He levered himself up, to look into her eyes as her body tightened further. As if he could sense she was close and he wanted to watch her take that wild ride.

"Come on, Emma, let go."

Then she did. What he'd made her feel only moments ago, paled in comparison to what exploded within her body now. She shrieked his name, clung to him and moved with the force of the climax slamming into her. It seemed to roll on and on, taking her higher and higher and Caden kept her firmly tethered to him while she soared. Finally, after what felt like forever, she heard him shout her name and when his body shattered, she clung to him, and they took the hard fall together.

A few minutes later, Caden had to silently admit that he felt energized in a way he hadn't in far too long to think about. Making love with Emma again had felt like...coming home. The two of them shared a connection he'd never found with anyone else. And while his body was happy, his mind was racing with all kinds of warning bells and a tiny voice shouting *red alert*!

He didn't need that voice, though. He already knew that sex with Emma solved nothing. Changed nothing. There were still five long years between them and the betrayal that had begun it all. That he couldn't bring himself to forget.

She was home now, but for how long? Was she just here in Montana as a pit stop before hitting the road again? How was he supposed to know? How could he ever trust her again?

He rolled away from her onto his back and tossed one arm across his eyes. Beside him, he heard her breath rushing in and out of her lungs and felt the heat of her body reaching out for him.

And he wanted her again.

To fight that urge, he got out of bed, crossed to

the bathroom to clean up, then gave himself a hard-eyed stare in the mirror. *Remember who you're dealing with*, he warned himself. *Keep your guard up.*

"Caden?" Her voice, still slightly breathless, called to him. "Everything okay?"

Still glaring at himself, he answered, "Fine."

He stepped out of the bathroom and paused on the threshold, looking at the bed where Emma lay sprawled across the mattress. She was a wonder, he thought idly, as he might if he were looking at a beautiful painting.

Her tantalizing mouth was curved in a secretive smile and that amazing hair of hers spilled across his pillows and then drifted down across her breasts, giving her nipples a peekaboo effect.

Her body was slim and strong, and if he didn't know she'd had a baby just a few months ago, he'd never have guessed. A baby. Emma had a daughter. She'd gotten pregnant by some other man. A rush of fury filled him, then drained away again. Who was he? *Where* was he? Why had she run from him?

"Wow," she mused softly. "For a man who just got lucky, you don't look very happy."

He blew out a breath. "Sex doesn't change anything, Emma."

She went up on her elbows, cocked her head to one side and said, "I don't know. I think it changed *something*." Pushing higher up, she stretched her arms over her head in a slow, languorous movement that sent Caden's gaze to her breasts, still peeking through the long silky curls of her hair.

His body stirred and he looked down at his own dick as if it were a traitor. The problem was, he considered, that a man's penis didn't give a damn what he was *thinking*. It only *wanted*.

And his wanted Emma. Now.

Her gaze dropped to his erection and that smile on her mouth curved higher. "Looks like at least a part of you agrees with me."

"At least you didn't say a 'small' part of me," he drawled and could have bitten off his own tongue when she laughed.

Damn, he'd missed that laugh. Musical, deep, infectious. Emma had always thrown herself into laughter and Caden had spent a huge amount of time trying to make her laugh just so he could listen to it. Now she was here, in his house, in his bed, and he was silently arguing with himself about what this would mean going forward.

Well, who the hell cared?

Enjoy what you had while you had it and let go of the rest of it.

With that thought firmly in mind, he absently flipped a switch alongside the fireplace and heard the gas flames kick into life. She sighed and that soft sound fed the heat inside him until Caden was sure he would simply spontaneously combust.

That burning need forced him across the room in

a damn hurry. He was drawn to her like metal shavings to a magnet. He always had been. Emma was the one thing in his life that had always defied description. What she was to him was too complex to label and too overpowering to ignore.

The light in the room was fading, but she seemed lit from within. Firelight danced across her bare skin, flickering shadows that defined every curve. Emma was watching him and her green eyes shone with anticipation as he paused long enough to grab a fresh condom and slide it on. He'd spent a lot of sleepless nights over the past five years, thinking about this moment. This woman. *No more thinking.*

He turned to her and she smiled up at him, lifted her arms in welcome and parted her lips for his kiss. He took what was offered and claimed her mouth with his. The taste of her exploded and spread through him on a river of heat. Their tongues tangled in a frantic burst of need—need that roared and clawed at his insides as if that climax only moments ago hadn't happened.

Caden ran his hands up and down her body, then settled on those breasts that had been driving him crazy. He cupped them both and she sighed into his mouth. His thumbs moved across her hard, dark pink nipples and she shivered. Then he tore his mouth from hers and lowered his head to those beautiful breasts and the sensitive, rigid nipples that tempted him so.

First one, then the other, he kissed and licked and nibbled, loving the taste of her. The sound of her sighs. The choked-off whimper that shot from her throat when he dropped one hand to her center and cupped the damp heat there. Her hips moved against his hand as she rocked helplessly, reaching for release from the tension rocketing up inside them both.

Caden was nearly blind with need. He lifted his head, stared down into her eyes and smiled. She was his again. His for now. His for however long he could keep her in this bed.

"Caden," she whispered, still moving her hips restlessly, "enough with the foreplay. Be in me."

"Plan to," he assured her, then sat back.

"You're stopping again and it's making me crazy." Confused, she pushed her hair back and stared at him.

"Not stopping," he said tightly, reaching for her. "Just rearranging."

With one quick move, he flipped her onto her stomach and then cupped her behind with his palms. Squeezing, kneading, he watched her squirm, heard the catch in her throat as she said again, "Come on, Caden. You're killing me."

He laughed shortly. "That is *not* the plan."

How many times had he lain awake in bed, picturing this moment, remembering others? How many nights had he simply given up on sleep and stalked through the quiet dark house like a man looking for something to remind him he was alive? Now she was here, with him, and he couldn't get enough of her. Didn't think he'd *ever* have enough of her. And that should worry him, Caden thought. He couldn't trust her to stay. Couldn't believe that she was really *back*. So, as much as he wanted her, as much as he loved having her here, he wouldn't allow himself to feel again what had once been the driving force in his life.

He wouldn't love her again.

Wouldn't risk that again.

But he could be with her, take what she offered and give what he could.

Taking hold of her hips, he lifted her off the mattress and said softly, "Come up to your knees, Emma…"

She threw a quick, surprised look at him over her shoulder. Licking her lips, she did as he asked, moving slowly, deliberately. When she was on her knees, her gorgeous behind in the air, Caden moved in behind her. He held her butt still when she would have moved again and as she looked back at him, studying him through clear green eyes, Caden pushed his body into hers with one long, satisfying stroke.

She groaned and her fingers curled into the comforter. Tossing her head back, she moved into him as he took her with a fast, hard rhythm. Sighs and moans slid from her throat as he kept them both at a frantic pace. Again and again, he took her, reclaiming what had once been between them. Reminding her of what they'd had. Reminding her what she'd tossed aside. Reminding himself.

"Caden…" His name was a plea. A command. A wish. He heard all of that and more in her voice and he responded.

Reaching down between them, he used his thumb to stroke that hard nub of sensation at her center. And still, he slammed himself home over and over again, feeding the growing tension within him.

"Caden!" She screamed his name and it was like music. She pushed back against him, trembling, rocking, shuddering as her release crashed into her.

An instant later, Caden claimed his own prize and nearly howled as his body erupted into an avalanche of satisfaction.

Breathing wasn't easy. He collapsed onto the bed, keeping her pinned to him, her back to his front. Bodies still joined, he rode the last of those tremors, waiting for his heartbeat to slow.

Against him, she squirmed a little, creating another ripple effect of sensation. In response, Caden held her still. "Now you're killing me."

Chucking gently, she took a breath and let it out on a sigh. "That was…" Emma shook her head as if she couldn't find the right word for what they'd just experienced. He knew how she felt. Hell, he'd been with plenty of women since Emma left Montana. He'd found satisfaction with most of them, but he'd never known the kind of earth-shattering climax that was only found in her arms.

He could have hated her for that alone.

Why should she still have any kind of hold on him? Well, that was a question he'd asked himself a lot. To this day, he didn't have an answer.

"...new," she finally finished and it took him a second to connect that word to the beginning of her statement.

She turned her head on the pillow and looked back at him. "You've got some new moves since the last time we were together, Caden."

He couldn't help himself; he smoothed a long strand of dark hair from her eyes. "The world didn't stand still while you were gone, Emma. I didn't stand still, either."

He disentangled their bodies because he'd learned long ago that a conversation with Emma required him to focus. And how the hell could he concentrate on a conversation when he was already hardening inside her again? He got up, took care of the condom issue, then went back to his bed, lying down beside her, but separate.

She didn't let that stand for long. Turning around, she went up on her elbows and looked at him. He didn't have a clue what she was thinking. Emma had always been partly a mystery to him and maybe that had been a draw back in the day. It was exciting, never being able to predict what his woman would do from one moment to the next. But it didn't make for easy conversations.

"So where'd you learn all these new tricks?" she asked in a way-too-quiet voice. "My sister?"

He threw her a hot look. "What?"

"Gracie. You remember her, right?" Temper was sounding in her voice now and in response, Caden's did the same. "Are you having sex with my sister?"

"None of your business, Emma." How many times would he have to say that?

She sat up on and stared down at him. "Tell me. Should I be getting dressed and leaving to make room for my little sister? When's the shift change here?"

His gaze pierced hers. "You're being an idiot."

"And you're not denying anything."

"Because like I said, not your business."

"Gracie's my business," she argued.

"And she's my friend," he countered.

"I was your friend, too," she reminded him, "when we were having sex out in your barn."

Was she jealous? That thought almost made him smile but the daggers she was shooting him told Caden that would be a big mistake.

"You left, Emma. You don't get an opinion on what we did after you were gone."

"So you did do something." She nodded sharply and he wondered how a woman could look so dangerous and so appealing all at the same time. "And believe me when I say I really do have an opinion."

Hell, it was tempting to let this go on. To let her wonder and fuss over what was between him and Gracie. Didn't she deserve a little torture for what she'd put him through? After all, Caden had done plenty of wondering himself about what Emma was up to out in California. But even as he considered it, he let it go. Caden wasn't going to play games with her. And if he was, he wouldn't use Gracie to do it.

"Damn it, Caden..." She pushed him, both hands on his chest, as if demanding his attention.

He caught her hands in his. His gaze locked on hers. "We did nothing, Emma. *Nothing* is between me and Gracie. I'm her friend. That's all."

She studied him for a few long seconds before he could see the tension slide from her system. "Really?"

"Really." He let her go, pushed one hand through his hair and then bunched the pillow under his head. "When you left, she needed a friend and I was there. I'll always be there for her. Hell, she's as much *my* little sister as she is yours."

The last of her anger slid away. He watched her let it go and had to admit that as quickly as she was to boil, Emma could let it go just as fast. She didn't hold grudges. She apologized when she was wrong and she was someone he could always count on. Well, he corrected, she used to be.

"Okay," she muttered. "I'm sorry. I know she must have needed you and I'm grateful you helped her out."

Scowling at her, he said, "I didn't do it for you, Emma."

"I know that, but I still appreciate it." She blew out a breath. "And I'm really glad you didn't sleep with Gracie because that would just be too weird. With a huge side of *ew*."

He snorted. Trust Emma to make him laugh at the oddest moments.

"But there is something going on with her, isn't there?"

And just like that, he wasn't laughing anymore. Instead, he walked around the bed, grabbed his jeans and yanked them on.

When he didn't say anything, she just stared at him. "That nonanswer was actually an answer, you get that, right?"

He lifted his gaze to her and nearly tore his jeans off again. She looked like temptation personified. Sitting there, bare-ass naked, that glorious hair of hers spilling over her shoulders and across her breasts and those forest green eyes fixed on him.

"I didn't say a thing," he muttered, shaking his head in an attempt to clear it.

"Exactly. If there was nothing going on, you would have said so, but because you didn't, I know there *is* something she's not telling me."

"Amazing how you do that circle speak," he murmured, and tossed his shirt to her.

"I have my own clothes," she said as she caught it.

"Takes too long and I'm really hungry for those sandwiches now."

"And for changing the subject…"

"Well, I guess you *do* know me, don't you?"

"I do, so I recognize the tactics to throw me off."

He shoved both hands into his jeans pockets, rocked back on his heels and looked down at her. She was shrugging into his shirt and something about her wearing his clothes made him hard again. Hell, everything about Emma Williams made him hard. Damn it.

"I'm not talking about it," he ground out. "If Gracie wants you to know, she'll tell you."

"No, she won't. She's so mad I'm home, she only speaks to me when she's got a good barb to shoot my way."

He headed out of the bedroom, expecting her to follow and she did. He could feel her right behind him. Their bare feet didn't make a sound on the stair runner and as they walked down the long hall to the kitchen, Emma hurried to keep up.

"I'm worried about her, Caden," she admitted, grabbing his arm to pull him to a stop. "Is she in trouble? Can you at least tell me that?"

He could see the anxiety in her eyes and a small piece of the ice she'd draped over his heart so long ago chipped off and fell away. He understood worry for family and though Gracie's secret wasn't his to tell, he could give Emma this. "She's not in trouble. She's just working some stuff out. When she's ready, she'll tell you."

"There was a time she told me everything," Emma mused quietly.

"Times change," he said.

"Yeah, I know that. And I know it's because of me. Doesn't make it any easier to accept."

He walked on toward the kitchen and Emma kept step with him. How many times had he pictured her here, in this house that his dream had built?

Now she was here—but he didn't trust her to stay.

Six

At the Little River Diner, Gracie sat across from Madison in a window booth at the back. The wall of windows showcased the river that ran through Cache and the trees that shrouded it. Aspens were bright gold and the maples were a deep scarlet. The pines were a rich, dark green and the diner felt as if it was in a secluded forest rather than at the edge of a bustling small town.

The diner itself had been in that spot for forty years. The wood tables had been polished so many times they were as smooth as glass. The red booth seats were comfortable, inviting people to sit and stay for a while and sooner or later, the whole town passed through this small restaurant, so it was a sure place to catch up on local gossip.

Shifting her gaze from the view to the woman across from her, Gracie silently admitted that she loved watching Madison. The way she grinned, the way she stirred her coffee long after it was cool enough to drink. The way she tucked stray strands of red hair behind her ear where silver leaves dangled from her lobes.

Since she first moved to Cache, Madison had become a sort of safe space for Gracie. She knew that she could tell Mad anything and it would be protected. She knew that her friend would always understand and would always be on her side.

"What're you thinking?" Madison took a sip of her coffee and waited.

"I was just thinking how glad I am that you moved to Cache."

"Hey, me, too." Reaching out, Madison grabbed Gracie's hand and squeezed briefly. "And, while you're still so pleased to have me, I'm going to test it by asking if you had a chance to talk to Emma after I left the ranch."

"Well, there went my nice little glow," Gracie muttered and slumped back against the booth. "No, I didn't. You saw her leave. And she hadn't come back by the time I left to meet up with you."

Madison shrugged. "Well, talk later tonight. Or tomorrow."

And say what? *You shouldn't have left?* What would be the point? "Talking won't solve anything."

"Nothing gets solved *without* talking."

"Boy," Gracie mused, with an accompanying eye roll, "I used to think Emma had the hardest head in the world. But you're coming in a close second."

Madison sighed in clear disappointment. "I just want you to get past this, Gracie."

"Why's it so important to you?" Madison had never even met Emma, so why did it matter so much to her what Gracie's relationship with her sister was?

"Because I care about you, dummy." Madison shook her head and pushed aside the plate that still held half of her turkey club sandwich. "Ever since your sister got home, you've been so tense it's ridiculous. You say you were furious and hurt when she left."

"I was." God, the sting of that was still so fresh, the wounds inside ached.

"Well, she's *back*, and you're still furious. It makes no sense, Gracie. The two of you are *family*." Madison took a breath, shook her head and added, "And family's everything."

Just like that, she felt terrible. She looked into the other woman's green eyes, saw pain there and knew she'd inadvertently made it worse. Mad had lost both of her parents in a car accident just before she'd moved to Cache. She didn't have siblings or aunts or uncles, so of course she would look at having a sister as being a gift.

Long ago, Gracie had felt the same way. But having family didn't mean everything was sunshine and roses all the time. And pretending otherwise was ridiculous.

"I'm sorry, Mad." She took a sip of her coffee. "I really am. I know how you feel about family. But sometimes, things can't be put back together even if you want them to."

"Especially not if you don't try."

"Really?" Frustrated, Gracie sighed. "This is my fault now? Just a couple of minutes ago, I was thinking that you were always on my side and how nice it was to be able to depend on that."

"I am on your side, Gracie. But that doesn't mean I won't call you on it when I think you're wrong." She set her coffee down and reached for Gracie's hand again. Holding on, she said, "You're important to me. I want you happy. And I don't think you will be as long as this war with Emma is going on."

She pulled her hand free, crossed her arms over her chest and tried not to notice that she was acting like a child. "So I should end it? I didn't start it."

"Does that really matter?"

She thought about that for a long minute before admitting, "Yeah. It does." Gracie saw the disappointment on Mad's face, and ordinarily would have tried to wipe it away. But now, she just wanted her to understand. To see things the way Gracie did.

"My whole life, Emma was—I don't want to say a role model, because how lame does that sound—but

I looked up to her. Trailed around after her." Gracie sat forward, pushed her own roast beef sandwich aside and leaned both forearms on the table. "When our mom died, I felt lost, but Emma stepped right in. She's five years older than I am and she just... became Mom, in a way. She made sure Dad and I were eating right, made sure I got to school, and she handled most of the ranch jobs alone because Dad was shattered."

"I know, you've told me," Madison whispered.

"Then she left, Mad." Gracie shook her head and glanced out the window. The diner sat alongside the river and she noticed the jewel-toned leaves were now whipping into the air as the wind kicked up. Shifting her gaze back to the woman across from her, Gracie said, "It was like Mom died all over again. One day Emma was there and the next she was gone. She'd been taking care of everything and suddenly, she wasn't. There was another empty hole on the ranch and this time there was no one to fill it."

"*You* filled it, Gracie."

A reluctant smile curved her mouth at the pride in Madison's voice. But she hadn't been in Cache back then so she didn't know how badly Gracie had stumbled. How she'd gone through the days blind and lost, trying to figure out all of the things that Emma had done so easily. "Thanks, but I didn't step up right away. I didn't know what I was doing, Mad. I messed up. A lot. I had to learn overnight how to run the ranch. How to fire men who weren't doing the work. How to stand my ground with men who looked at me and saw a kid."

"But you did it," Madison said with just a touch of impatience in her voice now. "Everyone fails at first when they do something new. You're not a failure because you messed up. You're only a failure if you quit. If you stop trying.

"That's what you're not getting," Madison said, impatience now ringing in her voice. "You're holding on to all of this old anger at your sister because you were tossed into the deep end. But, Gracie, you learned to *swim*."

She didn't want to hear that. Didn't want to believe it, and would have said so, but Mad wasn't finished.

"If Emma hadn't left, maybe that wouldn't have happened. Maybe you wouldn't have realized that you're a smart, capable woman on your own." Madison smiled and shrugged. "And maybe… Emma leaving was the best thing that ever happened to you."

Her words were quiet, but the idea behind them was earth-shattering. Gracie had never thought of it like that before and she had to admit that Madison might have a point. Yes, she'd been in over her head at first, but she was the one who had kept the ranch running the past five years.

She'd started in on her own dream of providing

equine therapy by studying at the local junior college. She'd sold off some horses and bought others that would be a better fit for the clients she would start taking soon.

She'd learned how to take a stand with the foreman, with her father. She had done it all and no matter how hard things had gotten, no matter how many nights she'd lain in bed crying with frustration and fear and anger, Gracie hadn't run. She hadn't quit. She'd grown into a strong, confident woman and she had to wonder if any of that would have happened if Emma had stayed. Wouldn't she have simply stepped back and gone with the flow? Let Emma handle the big stuff and tried to find herself in bits and pieces?

A rush of pride swelled inside her and Gracie had to silently admit that it felt good. Madison had a point, she realized and wow, was that annoying. It was hard to acknowledge that maybe it was time to let go of being mad at Emma. She'd held that hurt and fury so close for five years, how would she feel without it?

"Gracie?"

She came up out of her thoughts to smile at the woman standing beside their table. Jessica Whitehead, the principal of the local high school, had grown up in Cache and gone to school with Emma. She was tall, with short black hair, sharp brown eyes and a ready grin.

"Hi, Jess," Gracie said, then nodded at Mad. "You know Madison, right?"

"Sure I do," Jessica said with a laugh. "My dogs know her much better, though."

"Nice to see you." Madison smiled. "How's Max's foot?"

Jess waved one hand. "Oh, he's fine, thanks to you. How he stepped on a bee is beyond me. My son's been taking care of him and Max is deliberately limping now to get extra treats."

Madison grinned. "Sounds right."

"So, Gracie," Jess said, "I heard Emma's back. Is it true?"

Gracie sighed a little, but nodded. "It's true."

"Is she just here on a visit?" Jess shrugged. "I ran into Stephanie Cramer in the grocery store and she said she thought Emma had moved back permanently, but I didn't know if I could believe the gossip or not."

"She says she's home to stay." And oddly, Gracie realized that she hoped Emma meant it.

Jess gave a huge sigh of relief. "Oh, good. When you see her, would you ask her to call me?"

"Sure. What's going on?"

"It's complicated," Jess hedged, "but I might have a job for her, if she's interested."

Gracie blinked at her. "A job?"

"Just ask her to call me, will you?" Lifting one hand to both of them, she said, "Good to see you guys. I've gotta run. My husband's out in the car, ready to get our date night going. We're headed to Kalispell for a movie."

"Have fun," Madison said as Jess hurried off.

"A job," Gracie muttered, shaking her head in disbelief. "She's gone five years, shows up out of nowhere, flowers, balloons, cheers from the crowd, and then presto—a job."

"Don't look now," Madison pointed out, "but you're sounding bitter again."

Still irritated, she snapped, "And why wouldn't I?"

Madison glanced out the window. "Hey, it's snowing."

Gracie's gaze went right to the window. Snowflakes were flying along with the autumn leaves now and the snow was coming in thick. October snow wasn't all that unusual in Montana, especially at their elevation. But this sudden burst of thick flying snow made Gracie think it would soon turn into a big storm. "We'd better get going."

"Right." They left money on the table for the bill and tip, then hurried out to the parking lot.

The wind was like a frozen knife, slicing right through them both and driving down to the bone. Madison tugged her hand-knit, bright red hat down low on her head and looked at Gracie.

"It's already coming down so hard, why don't you just stay at my place in town tonight?"

Gracie pulled on her own hat, then shoved her hands into her coat pockets. "No, I'd better get back to the ranch." She threw a worried glance at the sky and got a face full of snow for her trouble. Shaking her head, Gracie said, "Dad's alone there with the baby."

"Emma might be home by now."

"She might," Gracie acknowledged, "but I can't count on her. I've got to make sure everything on the ranch is okay and ready for the storm."

"Don't look now, but you're still in charge."

"Really?" Gracie shook her head. "An I-told-you-so right now?"

Madison shrugged and smiled. "Couldn't resist."

Laughing, Gracie said, "Fine. Point made. Again. I've got to go, before this gets worse."

"All right." Madison nodded, then stepped up and gave Gracie a hard, tight hug. "Just be careful, okay? And text me to let me know you got home safely."

Gracie hugged her back, then let her go. "I will. And don't worry. I've been driving these roads in all kinds of weather since I was a kid."

Helplessly, Madison shrugged. "I'll worry anyway."

Gracie grinned. "I will, too. So get home safe. I'll text you."

The ride to the ranch was harrowing and it seemed with every passing minute, the snow got thicker and the wind harder. Her windshield wipers were barely up to the task of keeping the glass clear and Gracie held the wheel in a white-knuckle grip. By the time she turned into the drive at the ranch, the snow was so thick she could barely see.

A sudden blizzard wasn't surprising, but it was a pain in the ass. She hoped the ranch hands had gotten all the horses into the stable—and she'd be checking on that herself as soon as she made sure her dad was all right. But the first thing Gracie noticed as she parked and jogged to the front porch was that Emma's car wasn't parked where it had been. Which meant she wasn't home yet. And judging by this storm, she wouldn't be turning up anytime soon.

From the porch, Gracie turned and looked out at the swirling wall of white blowing over the yard. For the first time in five years, she felt worried for her sister.

Caden walked into the kitchen and realized the room was dark. How long had they been upstairs? He hit the light switch and the hanging copper-and-glass pendant lamps over the island blinked into life.

His beer was warm, so he got a new one for both of them and then sat down beside her to grab a sandwich. For a few minutes there was an almost companionable silence between them. But Emma had never been one to appreciate quiet for long. Now was no different.

"How did you do it?" she asked.

"What?"

"Build this place." She swept one arm out as if to

encompass the whole house. "I was only gone five years. How did you manage all of this so quickly?"

He could have ignored the question on the grounds that she'd given up her right to know about his life. But why shouldn't she know that he'd succeeded? That his life had marched on without her? Besides, he was damned proud of what he'd accomplished.

He shrugged. "I found gold."

She choked on a sip of beer and slapped her hand against her chest as she coughed violently. Holding up one hand when he tried to help, she fought for breath. When she finally could speak, she only said, *"Gold?"*

He nodded, satisfied at her reaction. Hell, he'd been nearly that surprised himself. "Remember how my dad used to talk about all the gold that was still up in the mountains waiting to be discovered?"

"Of course I do," she said, taking a sip of her beer. "The summer I was sixteen, we rode up to the high country a couple of times a week, looking for lost gold mines."

He smiled at the memory, then let it go. Because they hadn't spent all of their time looking for gold. Up in the mountains, they'd had picnics and sex in the sunshine and skinny-dipping in the lake, which led to more sex and then once, even sex on horseback.

Memories filled him, taunting him with images of Emma, reminding him what they'd had, what they'd lost. Finally, Caden deliberately shut his treacherous brain off.

Taking a long sip of his beer, he set the bottle down onto the granite and looked at Emma. Her hair was a wild tumble, her eyes were shining, and her delicious mouth was curved in a half smile that tugged at something deep inside him. Looking at the beautiful woman next to him, he could still see the girl that had driven him crazy.

Getting a grip, he said, "Well, when you left, I spent that spring riding the ranch." He'd needed to be by himself. To be away from every place that reminded him of the woman he'd loved and lost. The problem was, he acknowledged now, almost every square inch of the ranch was imprinted with her memory. He saw her everywhere and had felt her loss as he would have a limb. So he had lost himself in a hunt for the gold that could change his life. Build his dreams.

Caden forced a half-hearted laugh. "It got to the point where I swear my horse tried to hide from me every morning."

"Caden..."

"Not an accusation," he said, cutting her off. He didn't want another damn apology that changed nothing. "I'm just telling a story." His gaze locked with hers. "Do you want to hear it or not?"

"Really do," she said, picking up her beer for another sip.

Nodding, he kept his gaze locked on hers and

said, "You'd been gone a month when I found a nugget in the river."

"A single nugget didn't do all of this," she interrupted.

One dark eyebrow lifted. "Am I telling this or not?"

"Sorry." She held up a hand. "Go ahead."

Shaking his head, he curled his fingers around the cold beer bottle and twirled it absently in the wet ring it had made on the granite. "I found the nugget, figured it had washed downstream."

"Makes sense."

Nodding still, he said, "So I followed the river, found a few more small nuggets, and finally after a few weeks I stumbled across the source." Smiling to himself, Caden remembered that flush of success when he'd spotted the thick vein of gold behind an outcropping of rock. It was a stray ray of sunlight glittering on the golden surface that had caught his eye. Without that extra splash of light, he might have ridden right past it.

"Anyway I didn't have much equipment with me, but I hacked out a bit more, took it into Kalispell and had it appraised. Came back almost eighty-four percent pure."

"Wow."

"Yeah." He laughed shortly. "That was pretty much my reaction. And the appraiser's. Said he never saw raw gold that pure. It was 20k gold and I'd found a thick vein of it on the property."

"That's amazing, Caden." She reached out to lay one hand on his forearm and he glanced down. He liked the feel of her hand on his arm and for that reason moved away from her touch.

"It was. Dad laughed his ass off when I told him about it." He chuckled a little at the memory. "You know how he loves being right."

"I do. So what happened next?"

Caden shrugged, took a drink of his beer and looked at her. "A couple months later, I went back with Jack and we took out more."

"A couple of months? Why'd you wait so long to go back—" She broke off, and looked at him suspiciously.

"I had a lot to do here," he said flatly, avoiding her gaze. "Jack and I were working on the plans for this place, helping my folks move to Texas…"

"All good reasons," Emma said, and her mouth twitched as she tried to hide a smile. "But that's not why you waited, is it?"

Caden scowled at her, but Emma's smile only got brighter and her eyes sparkled in the overhead lights.

"You couldn't find it again," she said with a laugh in her voice. "Oh, my God. You got lost coming back to the ranch the first time so you couldn't remember where the gold was!" Her laughter spilled out into the room. "You never did have a sense of direction!"

He sighed and took a moment to enjoy the sound of her laughter. Emma had always teased him about his ability to get lost on his own damn ranch. And it felt…good, to hear it again. Though he still said, "This isn't funny."

"Sure it is."

"Anyway…" He ignored the last of her chuckles and grasped hold of what dignity he could find. "We pulled in enough out of that one vein to build this place, stock it with horses and set my folks up with a smaller spread in Texas."

"That's a heck of a story," she said at last and he waited, sure there would be more. He wasn't disappointed.

"You're still the only cowboy I know who can get lost on his own ranch."

"I don't get lost," he corrected. "I get *turned around*."

"Turned around," she said, perfectly in time with him.

Irritated, he took another swig of beer. "Funny."

She laughed. "It's what you always said."

"Not anymore. That almost never happens now. Besides, I've always found my way well enough. Seems to me you're the one who's been lost."

Just like that, her smile died and her eyes went cool. "I guess you're right about that. I have felt lost for a long time."

"And now you're back," he said. "And you're having all your questions answered… Now it's my turn."

"What's that supposed to mean?"

Before he could ask his question, someone pounded on the back door just before it swung open.

A blast of cold air rushed into the kitchen, followed by Jack Franklin, who swept off his hat and slapped it against his thigh, sending a tiny blizzard of snow to the floor. "Sorry, boss." He nodded. "Emma. Big storm blew in in the last half hour or so. Thought you'd want to know."

"How bad?" Caden was already up and moving.

"Most of the horses are safe inside. A couple of the guys are bringing in the mares from the south pasture."

Nodding, Caden said, "Good. Send a couple more out to help. If the snow's too bad, they'll need it coming across the river."

"On it," Jack said, turning for the door again.

"I'll be out there in five minutes." He shot a look at Emma. "Make that ten."

"Right." The door closed and Jack was gone. Emma got up, went to the window and stared past the darkened glass to the wall of white beyond. "How could we not notice what was happening?"

He snorted. "We were busy."

"Yeah." She threw him a quick look. "I've gotta get back."

"No way in hell, Emma." He said it flatly, brooking no argument. "Not even you can navigate a road you can't see."

"I know every bump in that road, Caden. I need to get home. Help Gracie. Check on Molly and Dad."

"Call 'em," he ordered. "No point in you crashing or getting stuck. That won't help your family any."

She really hated it when he was right. "Okay. I'll stay. I'll get coffee on and make soup or something for you and the guys." He nodded, already heading out of the kitchen, stalking down the hall. Emma was right behind him. "Once I've got it going, I'll come out and help in the stable."

He whirled around, looked down at her, then yanked her to him, planted a fast, hard kiss on her mouth, before letting her go. "All right."

Swaying a little, Emma stared after him as he took the stairs, then she fell into step. They had to get dressed and take care of business. Everything else would just have to wait.

It only took a minute or two for Caden to dress and then he was gone. Emma picked up her cell phone and walked to the windows overlooking the front of the ranch and hit speed dial. Staring out at the swirling rush of white, she shook her head. Caden was right. Nobody should be driving in this.

"Emma?" her father said when he answered. "You all right?"

"Yeah, Dad. But it looks like I'm stuck here at Caden's until the storm blows out."

"Good. I was worried you'd try the road. No need."

"But Molly..." Guilt. She'd brought the baby home with her and she should be there caring for Molly herself. She had never intended to hand off responsibility for her to the family.

"Molly's fine. We'll keep her safe and warm. You

do the same for yourself." That was an order, too, not a request, and Emma realized she had a couple of men in her life who had no problem dishing out commands. And she had no problem arguing with them. When it made sense.

"I will. Is Gracie okay?"

"Got home just a while ago," her father said. "She's fine. Out in the barn helping the men bring in the horses."

"Okay, then." Emma nodded to herself. Everyone was safe. That was the important part. "I'll call again in the morning. But if you need me, call and I'll find a way there."

"We're fine," her father said again. "You just sit tight and take care of you and Caden."

When he hung up, she looked down at the ranch yard and watched Caden and another of the cowboys getting a couple of horses moving to the stable. Even in the rush of snow, she had no trouble picking Caden out of a crowd. She never would. If her eyes couldn't do it, her heart could.

And now was a hell of a time to admit to herself that she was still in love with the cowboy of her dreams.

Seven

I'm home. Everything's good. Emma's staying at Caden's till after the storm.

Gracie hit Send and waited, hoping Madison would answer right away. When she did, Gracie smiled.

Be careful. I'm fine, too. And I'm in for the night unless that cow has other ideas.

Frowning, Gracie texted back.

Let the cow handle her own problems. You're not used to driving in snow like this.

A moment later, Don't worry so much.

But Gracie was worried. She looked out the open stable door at the wall of icy white outside and shivered. This kind of storm could blow out in a couple hours or settle in for days. No one knew what would happen, not even the weather guy on TV who had predicted mostly cloudy skies today.

"Gracie! Need some help over here!"

She shoved her phone into her back pocket and rushed down the wide center aisle to the stall at the back. Her latest purchase, a gelding named Herman of all things, was refusing to go inside. So she'd take care of business, help her father with the baby and hope that Emma and Madison stayed safe.

An hour later, she was in the house, looking for hot coffee, and found her dad in the kitchen with the baby.

"Where'd you find the high chair?" Gracie asked, watching Molly slap both hands on the tray in front of her.

"Up in the attic," Frank said. "Your mom never threw out anything that her girls used."

True. Somewhere in that attic was every report card, every history paper and even a few stuffed animals that Gracie and Emma had outgrown. A swell of regret filled her when she looked at Molly and realized how much Gracie's mom would have loved having a baby in the house again.

Heck, *she* was enjoying it. Molly was happy, always smiling and seeing what a miracle the baby had brought to Gracie's father was especially endearing.

"I've got her tied into the chair," Frank was saying. "She can't really sit up well on her own yet, but that'll come, won't it, Nugget?" He tapped Molly's nose with his index finger and the tiny girl laughed in delight.

Gracie poured a cup of coffee and looked around the large, familiar kitchen. The walls were still a sunshine yellow because that was what her mom had loved. The cabinets were white and the oak floor was scarred, but shining clean. The old table under the window had been the spot that she and Emma had gravitated to after school, for cookies, milk and homework.

"You're really enjoying this, aren't you?" Gracie dropped tiredly into a kitchen chair.

"Having my granddaughter in the house?" Frank asked, obviously surprised at the question. "'Course I am. About time you girls started giving me grandkids to spoil." He winked at Gracie. "It'll be your turn soon."

She only frowned and looked down into her coffee to avoid meeting her father's gaze. "Hard to do it on your own," she muttered.

"Oh, you'll find someone when the time's right."

She risked a glance at him and wondered what he'd say if she told him her secret. If she took the risk and let him know what she'd been hiding for too long. But how could she chance it? He was only now looking healthy again. For so long, he'd been sliding into a depression, and now that Emma and yes, Molly, had come home, he was like a new man. Did she really have the right to throw something at him that might set him back again?

"Everything all right, Gracie?" Frank sat down at the table opposite her. "Your face is telling me something's on your mind." His soft, understanding gaze was locked on her and she could only shift uncomfortably.

She hated lying to her father, but she wasn't ready to take a step from which there was no coming back.

"Yeah, Dad. I'm fine." Gracie forced a smile and made herself believe it. "I just needed some coffee, then I'm headed back out there. We've still got a few horses to bring in and I want to make sure they've all got fresh feed and water."

"All right." He nodded and set a few slices of banana on the baby's tray.

Instantly, Molly's little hands curled around them and smushed them completely. Then she licked the mess from her fingers, spreading it all across her face.

"You're happy, aren't you?" Gracie whispered, looking from that sweet baby to her father.

"'Course I am," Frank said, reaching out to pat his youngest daughter's hand. "I've got my girls and this little nugget. What more could a man ask for?"

Nodding again, Gracie told herself she was doing the right thing by keeping quiet. Her secrets would have to stay buried deep—at least for now. She took a long drink of her coffee, then set the cup down. "I'd better get back."

"You tell the boys I've got some beef stew going. When they need it, just come on over and get it."

"Wondered what smelled so good," she said, taking a deep breath of the wonderful, steamy air. "I'll tell them."

And the men would be expecting it. At times when the whole crew was working nonstop, the big house always provided a hot meal and hot coffee to keep everyone going.

"Tastes even better." Frank winked and gave Molly more bananas to smush. "You come in to eat, too."

"I will." She turned to leave, but paused for one more look at her father and the baby. It wasn't fair, considering how hard she'd worked the past five years to keep this ranch alive, to keep her father going—that it was Emma and her daughter that had brought everyone back from the brink.

But as that thought settled in, Gracie pushed it out again and remembered Mad telling her she was being bitter and deliberately clinging to her own anger. It didn't really matter what had turned things around, did it? Wasn't the important thing that her father was better? That the ranch had someone else now to help care for it?

Some of the anger she'd been carrying around in her heart slowly drained away and it was simply amazing how much lighter she felt. Not that she was ready to throw her big sister a party or anything, but she was willing to give her the benefit of the doubt. If Emma was here to stay, then Gracie would just try to be happy about it. And if her sister up and left again? Well then, she'd survive. As she had before.

And with any luck, her father would continue to get stronger and someday soon, she could reveal her own secrets without risking the loss of those she loved.

For hours, Emma worked side by side with Caden and it was like old times only better. When they were younger, he'd had more of an I'm-in-charge-do-what-I-tell-you-to-do attitude. Naturally, she hadn't paid any attention to *that*, so they'd butted heads more often than not. Now, though, things were more equal between them as they worked together to get the horses in and secure for the night.

The storm kept raging and in just a couple of hours almost a foot of snow covered the ground. With the wind howling, Emma felt frozen to the bone. Cowboys took turns going into the kitchen in shifts for hot soup and coffee. By the time the work was done and everyone settled in for the night, she was exhausted.

Emma was also proud. She'd stood her ground and proved that those years in Hollywood hadn't changed the ranch girl inside. Spending time with the horses, calming them, feeding and watering them, had been nearly a spiritual experience. It brought back to her exactly what she'd figured out more than a year ago—this was where she belonged.

Now if she could just convince Caden that she also belonged with *him*. But sex wasn't commitment and when he looked at her, she could still see suspicion shining in his eyes. He was waiting for her to leave again. How long would it take to prove to him that she wasn't going anywhere?

With that depressing thought circling her mind, Emma stopped on her way to the house and though she was half-frozen, she paused long enough to enjoy what was happening. The air was silent and icy. The sky was obliterated in the wall of white rushing down. Snow settled on her eyelashes, her cheeks and her hair and she laughed with the glory of it. This was something she'd missed in California. The changing of seasons. The hush of winter snow. Now she was back and it felt right.

"Are you crazy?"

She turned to look at Caden and smiled. "Maybe, but this is beautiful."

"*You're* beautiful," he murmured and her eyes

widened. Before she could enjoy it, though, he added, "And frozen. Come on."

He took her hand and pulled her toward the back door. They dumped their coats and hats in the mudroom, stomped the snow off their boots and brushed it off their jeans before walking into the warm kitchen. There was a stack of dirty bowls and utensils in the sink, melting, snowy footprints on the floor, and the scent of the beef soup still hung in the air.

Shaking his head, Caden said, "We'll worry about kitchen duty tomorrow."

"Sounds like a plan," she said, because honestly, even the thought of trying to clean up tonight made her want to lie down and weep. On the other hand, the thought of lying down with Caden, wrapping herself around him, made her feel downright perky. "You want more soup?"

"No," he said and went to the fridge for a beer. "You want one?" he asked. "Or wine?"

"Wine. Definitely." Emma sat down on one of the stools and watched him get their drinks. Working with him had been good. They'd reawakened the rhythm they used to have and made Emma think that maybe, even if they couldn't go back, they could rebuild what they'd once had.

He handed her the wine, then took a seat across from her and had a long pull of his beer. Shoving one hand through his hair, he said, "Thanks. For the help tonight and for the soup. The guys appreciated it."

"You're welcome." Well, weren't they being polite? The camaraderie she'd felt earlier was quickly draining away and she didn't know how to get it back.

A second or two of silence passed with the two of them staring at each other across the center island. He was studying her, and the look in his eyes wasn't what she'd hoped to see.

"Had plenty of time to think tonight," he said, his voice quiet, thoughtful, "while we were getting the horses tucked away."

"Yeah?" She felt as if she should be bracing for something, but how could she when she didn't have a clue what it was he'd been thinking about? Was he going to tell her he didn't want to see her again? Tell her he still loved her, but would never trust her? She had a stomach full of raucous butterflies inside her going absolutely nuts.

"We've done a lot of talking since you've been here and that's fine. But what I keep coming back to is one thing, Emma."

"What's that?"

"You left because you said you had to chase your dreams and that didn't leave room for getting married or having a family." He set his beer down on the countertop and idly twisted it in circles. "But when you come home you've got a baby. Now, what am I supposed to think about that?

"Who's Molly's father? Who were you willing to have a family with, Emma?"

"Caden—" Those butterflies in her stomach became dragons. She'd come home with a secret and he was asking her to share it. But if she wanted him to trust her again, didn't *she* have to trust in him, too?

"No stalling." He shook his head and locked his gaze on hers, making it impossible for her to look away. "I answered your questions earlier today," he reminded her. "Now answer mine. Tell me about that baby."

In a way, she wasn't surprised that he was asking about Molly. Emma had known when she came home that eventually she'd have to tell people the truth. Especially Caden. There was just no way the man she loved would calmly accept, without an explanation, that she'd left him only to have a child with someone else.

But damn it, this had been a *good* day. She and Caden were, if not back together, at least not at open war with each other anymore. She didn't want to lose that. But if she didn't talk, wasn't she risking losing him anyway?

As soon as that thought scuttled through her mind, though, something else stood up, demanding to be recognized. Emma had to protect that baby no matter what. And if she were to open the box and let the secrets out, how could she keep Molly safe?

Shaking her head, she said firmly, "I'm really

sorry, Caden. Believe me, I am. But I can't talk about Molly."

He scrubbed both hands over his face, inhaled sharply and stood up. Coming around the end of the counter, he loomed over her, and Emma had to tip her head back just to meet those glittering blue eyes of his.

"Damn it, Emma. You owe me this. You left me, found yourself someone else and had *his* baby."

She could see the anger in his eyes, but beyond that, she saw hurt, and that she couldn't stand.

"Then you left him, too," he continued. "So what the hell is going on with you? Enough secrets, Emma. Tell me."

She looked up into his eyes, firing with hurt and anger and frustration. His entire body was tense and his jaw muscles twitched he was grinding his teeth so hard. Her heart ached because she'd never meant to hurt Caden. She was just trying to do the right thing.

"Stop thinking, Emma. Hell, I can almost hear your brain spinning." He grabbed her shoulders and held on. "Just say it."

"Molly's not mine."

"Well, find her." Dorian Baxter's voice was cold, sharp and impatient.

His assistant—what was his name? Ted? Tom? *Tim*—jolted.

"We're looking, sir," Tim said quickly. "We think she's gone home to Montana."

Dorian Baxter was forty-five years old, at the top of his game in Hollywood and had the biggest stars in the world on speed dial. He wasn't used to being placated and wouldn't accept it now. "You *think*?"

Another jolt from the younger man and this time the assistant took a step back, toward the door. Dorian noticed and told himself that it must be time for a different assistant. Why the hell hadn't he hired another woman? At least when a woman was giving him grief, she was better to look at.

"The investigator is on it, sir," Tim said, checking his notes briefly. "But apparently, there's a big snowstorm and he can't get out of the airport yet."

"Snow? Why the hell does anyone want to live in *snow*?"

"I don't know, sir."

"Of course you don't know. You don't know a hell of a lot." Dorian came out from behind his desk and only took a small zip of pleasure from the way Tim scooted farther out of his way.

He'd been on edge since the night before when he got the tip from a reporter he kept on his payroll. Someone had talked to another so-called "journalist" who was busy chasing down a lead that could bury Dorian if he didn't kill it first. He had to find the damn woman before this story made the papers. In *this* climate, he'd be crucified by a bunch of screaming women demanding his head and he wasn't going to go down like that.

His office, sitting high above Hollywood Boulevard, was an airy, modern place with chrome and glass being the main decorative statement. Chrome frames on the wall displayed posters from his award-winning movies. His desk was the most imposing piece of furniture in the room—as it should be. Careers were made and broken from behind that desk. And on either corner of that desk were the two Best Picture awards that his movies had won. Dorian had worked too hard and too long and kissed way too many butts to get where he was and damned if he'd give it up.

"You tell that guy to get his ass out on the road. I don't care if he has to rent a snowplow to do it. I need to know where that bitch went." Dorian glared at Tim and watched the man pale. Stabbing his index finger toward him, he said, "That article's going to run in another week and I want this sewn up before then. You understand me?"

"Yes, sir. I'll get right on it."

Dorian turned his back on him in a clearly dismissive gesture, then walked to the closest window. He stared down at the ants streaming down sidewalks, driving along the streets. He had this city by the balls and he wasn't about to give up any of it.

"I want this taken care of. I want answers and I want them yesterday."

"Yes, sir." Tim scuttled out of the office, leaving Dorian alone to muse over his lifestyle, his power and all that he'd managed to achieve.

No stupid bitch was going to ruin this for him.

Emma slapped one hand over her mouth the second she blurted out the words. But it was too late. Her secret was out now and the way Caden was looking at her in stunned surprise told Emma that there was no going back.

"What the hell does that mean?" He let her go and threw both hands in the air. "If Molly's not yours, why do you have her? Why does your dad think she's his granddaughter? And what aren't you telling me?"

Oh, God. Emma took a deep, shaky breath and still her head felt light. To either help with that or make herself pass out, she picked up her wine and took a healthy swallow. Dutch courage, as her grandfather used to call it. Whatever, she appreciated the low burn the wine left in her system, fighting the arctic cold now pouring from Caden's eyes.

"I can't believe I'm telling you this."

"You haven't told me much," he countered, then grabbed his beer and took a drink. "So why don't you just dive right in and get it all out? You said Molly's not yours. Explain."

Her throat felt tight, so she lifted one hand to the base of her neck as if she could dislodge the knot of emotion inside. "It means just what you think it means. I didn't give birth to Molly. My roommate, Terry Stone, did."

He backed up a step, shaking his head as if trying to make sense of the insensible. Rubbing one hand across the back of his neck, he demanded, "Well, where's Terry Stone and why did she give you her baby?"

"Terry's dead," Emma said and her voice broke on those two words. Because months-old memories enlarged that knot in her throat until she felt as if she was going to really choke. Images rose up in her mind, of Terry, curled up in a chair in their apartment. She hadn't wanted to eat, to go anywhere, to take care of the baby. Nothing could reach her because she'd withdrawn so deeply inside herself.

"Emma," he said and this time, his voice was lower, softer. "Talk to me."

Another sip of wine, another deep breath and Emma murmured, "Terry got pregnant by a big producer who told her if she slept with him, he'd put her in his new movie."

Caden looked furious at that piece of news. Well, Emma knew how he felt. She'd seen it too many times in Hollywood. Powerful men using young, hopeful, naive women, then tossing them aside for the next one in line. Terry had probably been one of hundreds.

"But he didn't, of course. He used her, then hired someone else for the movie." Battling the tears that blossomed in her eyes, Emma continued. Now that she'd finally started telling the story, she didn't think she'd have been able to stop even if she'd wanted to. "Terry was so ashamed. So shaken. Then the bastard spread the word in town that anyone who hired her would go straight to his enemies list. She couldn't get a job. Her agent dropped her. Then she discovered she was pregnant and she went back to Mr. Powerful and told him."

"He didn't help."

It wasn't a question. "No, he didn't. He gave her five hundred dollars to 'take care of it.'"

Caden's eyes flashed and his hands fisted at his sides.

She took a deep breath and admitted, "That's what broke her finally, I think. She didn't talk about it again and all during her pregnancy, she just sort of drifted. We worked at the same diner as waitresses, so I kept an eye on her as much as I could. But I couldn't *reach* her. Couldn't make her see that there was so much she could do. She could go home. Teach. She had her teacher's certificate, but she had dreamed her whole life of being a star."

"Like you," he said.

"Yes, like me," she agreed with a little disgust because she'd wanted the same thing that Terry had. Dreams were bright and shiny and appealing and when they splintered in your hands, you were blinded by the loss and couldn't see past the ruin to what could be. Hadn't she been blinded herself? Hadn't she stayed in Hollywood two years longer than she should have because leaving felt like more of a failure than staying?

Admitting you had failed was hard. For Terry, it had been *impossible*.

"What happened?" He came up close and smoothed a strand of hair back from her face. "Why do you have Terry's baby?"

She couldn't just sit there. Had to move. Being chased by her own thoughts, Emma pushed off the stool and started pacing the gigantic kitchen. She didn't see the beauty of it, she was simply grateful that it was big enough to give her plenty of room to move. Her insides were jumping, her mind was filled with images of Terry. The tiny apartment they'd shared. Of Molly.

Emma swiped tears off her cheeks with her fingertips and kept walking. Tears were useless. They couldn't change anything. Couldn't help Terry. Couldn't save her. And she'd never been the kind of woman to use tears to sway a man—or anyone for that matter. All she had to do was get through this.

She took a breath and started talking. "Once Terry had the baby I thought she'd be okay. She was totally in love with Molly—we both were. She was so tiny. So beautiful. And for a while, things were better. I was convinced that Terry had finally moved on."

She stopped, looked at Caden and said softly, "She

went to see Molly's father. I don't even know what she was hoping for. Interest? Love? Whatever it was, she was disappointed. She took a picture of the baby to show him and he had her thrown out without even seeing her. Told her through his assistant that if she ever came back he'd have her arrested for extortion."

In a split second, Caden muttered, "Sounds like a bastard."

"That's a generous name for him." She breathed deeply in an attempt to steady herself. It didn't really work, but she kept going anyway. "He knows enough powerful people that he could have made sure anything Terry might have said against him went away. And she knew it."

Wrapping her arms around her middle, she continued in a rush. This last bit would be the hardest. "Molly was four months old when Terry went out for a drive. I was babysitting because she needed to get out, clear her head.

"Later I found a letter she'd left for me and she said she was sorry, but she couldn't do it. Couldn't be the kind of mother her daughter deserved. Couldn't keep going on when there was just nothing left for her. She asked me to raise Molly and keep her away from her father."

Emma looked at Caden. "Terry didn't have any family, anyone else to count on, besides me. So when the police came and told me she'd died in a one car accident—she drove over a cliff in Malibu—I didn't say anything about the baby. I let them think Molly was mine. And a month later, I came home."

"So you came back because of the baby," he said finally.

Emma shook her head and met his gaze squarely, making sure he could see the truth on her face when she said, "No. I'd told Terry that I was moving back to Montana about a week before she died." More tears fell and she didn't bother to try to fight them. "I think that's why she did it. I think she knew that when I left, she'd be alone. She wouldn't have anyone to give a damn about her or Molly.

"So she killed herself and left Molly to me."

Eight

Caden was torn between dozens of different emotions.

Top of the list, though, were pity, fury, and finally, understanding. It was small of him to acknowledge, even to himself that he was damn glad Emma hadn't had a baby with some other man. That had been hard for him to accept and he didn't care if it did make him sound like a caveman or something. Knowing she'd rejected him and chosen someone else had been gnawing on him.

Now she was standing there, watching him and for the first time in her life, Emma Williams looked... vulnerable. She'd always been the strongest woman he'd ever known and seeing her unsure of herself was just wrong. Not to mention the fact that she was looking at him as if she were waiting for him to call the police and report her as a kidnapper.

"Jesus, Em. Relax. You did what you had to do. I'm not going to second-guess you on it."

She blew out a breath. "Thanks."

"Beyond that, I don't even know what to say about all this."

"That's okay. Neither do I." She took a shaky breath and straightened her shoulders, stiffened her spine. As he watched, the Emma he knew completely replaced the wounded woman she'd been only moments ago. "Weird, but I feel better after telling you all of it. It feels…good to get it out. To let someone know what I've been carrying around."

He walked over to her and dropped both hands onto her shoulders. She still felt cold from being outside, so he did what came naturally to him. He pulled her in close and wrapped his arms around her, giving them both the heat and the comfort they needed.

And while he held her, he asked the one question that was now uppermost in his mind. "Did he try to use you, too? That producer?"

"No," she said, and looked up at him. "But others did. He's not the only bastard in Hollywood."

Fury whipped through him like a lightning bolt and he held her even more tightly to him. Gritting his teeth, he asked, "Is that how you got that show you were on?"

"No!" She pushed away from him and stood there, with anger boiling in her eyes and simmering around her like a white-hot aura. "Is that what you think of me? That's I'd trade sex for a job?"

"No." Frustrated, he shoved one hand through his hair again. Of course he didn't think that, but hearing that story had made him want to go back in time and pummel that man and any other who would use a woman—especially Emma. "But—"

Clearly insulted, she said, "There shouldn't be a *but* in that sentence, Caden."

"There isn't," he said abruptly. "Not really. I was just mad at myself because I wasn't there when you needed me. Hell, if I know you, any man who tried that on you got kicked where it counts."

Her lips twitched and the fire in her eyes died to a smolder. "No, but I thought about it. Not every man in Hollywood is like that, though. There are a lot of decent people. But the reason I was a waitress for the last three years is because I refused to play the game," she snapped. Another deep breath and she held up one hand. "Sorry. It's just… It's so hard out there.

"Everyone's scrambling to make the right contacts, to be seen in the right places. You can't trust people like you do everywhere else. People in Hollywood are so insular, so worried about their own career or their next agent or the big audition. More worried about how things look than how they are.

It's easy to get caught up in it all and I can see why some do.

"I got that series job on my third audition." She shook her head ruefully. "I'd only been in Hollywood for two months. I'm not even sure why they hired me. Well, maybe partly because I was so new, they didn't have to pay me much. And because I hadn't been seen at a million auditions all over Hollywood. They were looking for 'fresh faces' and I guess I qualified." She gave a short laugh and even she winced at the bitter tone of it.

"It's a pretty nice face," Caden murmured.

"Thanks." She gave him a wry smile and then continued. "Anyway, I got the job, so for one season, I was the airhead astronaut in space and then the show got canceled after twelve episodes." She shrugged and sighed. "After that, almost every agent and casting director in town looked at me and said, 'Nope, too soon. You're typecast. Come back in a year. Or two. Or three.'"

"I didn't know." He gave himself a mental kick. He should have known. Should have made it his business to know. But he'd been too wrapped up in his own anger at her leaving to realize that things might not be going great for her. Caden would always regret that. "You never said."

"What was there to say?" She laughed, but it was a short, harsh sound, scraping from her throat. "The few auditions I *did* get, didn't go well. I was too tall or too short. My boobs were too big—"

"If it helps, I like them just fine."

She laughed again. "Or my hair was too long or too dark—had I considered going blonde?"

"No," he said, shaking his head. Her hair was gorgeous, tumbling dark curls with streaks of sunlight running through it. He wanted his fingers in it again, feeling that dark silk sliding across his skin.

"I have no butt—"

"Now I know they're crazy."

She grinned. "My favorite, though, was 'Your nose has a bump in it.'"

"I don't see a bump. It's a pretty nose."

"Thanks for the vote of confidence," she said wryly. "But going on auditions for a month will reduce your self-confidence to a mere shadow of its former self."

A woman as beautiful and talented and sexy as Emma should never doubt herself. He hated what they'd tried to do to her. "And yet, according to Gracie, you always talked about how great everything was."

"How could I tell them the truth?" she argued, throwing her hands up. "Was I going to call Dad and say, 'Hey, Hollywood sucks, the dream is dead and I'm a waitress at the Loa Loa Coffee Shop off Sunset'?" Shaking her head, she said, "I couldn't do that. He'd have worried himself sick."

"He did anyway," Caden pointed out.

Guilt washed over her features and he felt bad for reminding her. But truth was truth. If things had been that bad, what had taken her so long to come home?

"Yeah. I know that now. God I feel so stupid. But no one told me what was happening here." She pushed her hair back, folded her arms across her chest and said, "If I'd known, I'd have come home sooner. Trust me, the only thing keeping me there was not wanting to admit that I'd failed."

"Bullshit."

Surprised, she said, "What?"

"I call BS." Caden reached for her again. "I admit, I was pissed when you left."

"I know but—"

"Not finished," he said. "I was furious that you left me for some pipe dream of becoming a successful actor. But I'm not going to let you say you failed. You didn't, Em. You went for it. You chased it. You were on TV for God's sake."

"One season," she reminded him. "A short one at that."

He frowned at her. "More than most aspiring actors get, isn't it?"

She sighed and nodded. "Yes, I guess so."

Looking down at her, he gave her something else when he confessed, "And I thought you were really good."

Stunned, she stared at him. "You watched the show?"

He'd never admitted this to anyone before, but now seemed like the time to spill his own secrets. Hell, she needed it and if he wanted truth from her then he had to provide a few, too. "Yeah, I watched it. How could I not? I had to see if you'd done the right thing for yourself—and I'll admit this, too, that I was hoping you would suck at it. To prove that you should have stayed here. With me.

"I watched one episode. You were damn good, Emma." He huffed out a breath and said, "Seeing you on the TV, just shining and showing up every other actor in that stupid show—"

"It wasn't stupid," she countered with a low chuckle.

He lifted one brow. "Yeah, it was. But the fact that you could be that good in a show that bad only made me madder because I figured you'd proved that you were right to leave. So I never watched it again."

Emma smiled up at him and her green eyes glimmered in the overhead lights. "You know, I find that oddly flattering."

"You should," he told her and looked into those amazing eyes so she would see that he meant every word. "I almost tossed the television."

She laughed and he enjoyed hearing it rise up around him. "You were good, Emma. You didn't fail."

After a second or two, she asked softly, "Why are you being so nice to me?"

"Well," he hedged, "that's a question, isn't it?"

"And that's not an answer."

"No, it's not," he agreed. He wouldn't tell her he loved her still. Wouldn't say that having her back in Montana made the rest of his life straighten out. Wouldn't put his heart on the line because having it crushed once in a lifetime was more than enough. "Does it really matter?"

She sighed, moved in closer, laid her head on his chest and wrapped her arms around his waist. "No, it doesn't."

He tipped her face up to his, stared down into her eyes briefly, then lowered his head to hers and took her mouth fiercely. She clung to him, her tongue tangling with his and they swayed together, lost in the heat that flashed up between them. His body was on fire, his blood sizzled in his veins. She was everything. She was all. Her hands on him, his mouth fused to hers. This was what was important. The only important thing.

When he finally broke the kiss, his arms came around her and he held her tightly because he needed to feel her, safe and warm in his arms. Thinking about her alone in Hollywood used to haunt him. Now that he'd heard her story, he knew that he'd be haunted for a lot longer.

Two days later, Emma was back at her family's ranch. The snow had stopped, the sun was out and the temperature was rising enough that the fresh snow was melting as quickly as it had fallen.

When she got home, Molly greeted her as if she'd been gone a month and Emma's heart swelled with love for the baby girl. She hadn't given birth to Molly, but she'd been there with the baby since the day she was born. Emma *was* her daughter in every way that mattered. She didn't know what would happen in the future, but she knew she would fight for that baby no matter what. And now she had Caden on her side, as well.

Caden. Just the thought of him was enough to make her melt. She shivered, remembering all those hours wrapped around his body, feeling him moving deep within her. Her belly swirled with fresh desire and Emma didn't know how she'd make it through the day without touching him. So, the only thing she could do was to force her mind away from thoughts of him.

Her father was looking downright perky and even Gracie was a little less hostile. Emma was still finding her way back into the family circle, still a little unsure where she fit now, but at least she didn't feel as though she were trying to tiptoe her way across a minefield.

"Was Molly a lot of trouble?"

Gracie glanced at her. "I'd like to say yes, so I could make you feel guilty…but no. She was great. Dad loved taking care of her and I helped out when I could."

Emma leaned on the half stall door and watched

her sister using a currycomb on an older gelding. "I appreciate it, you know. If I could have gotten home from Caden's earlier, I would have."

Gracie paused, the comb resting on the horse's broad back. "Yeah. I know. And don't worry... I'll think of a way for you to pay me back."

"I'm sure." Emma was willing to take this conversation, since it was the friendliest one she'd had with her sister since coming home again. "So how long have you had this old boy?"

The horse lifted his head and gave Emma what would pass for a dirty look. She laughed.

"Hey, old is a state of mind and Herman's just getting started, aren't you?" Gracie stroked her hand down his back with a slow, gentle touch. The big animal turned his head to give Gracie a gentle nudge. "I brought him home a few months ago."

"Okay," Emma said, stepping into the stall and closing the door behind her. She picked up a brush and absently dragged it through Herman's mane. "Why?"

"He's good with kids. Patient. And—" Gracie ducked her head, shrugged, then said, "He's going to be one of my equine therapy horses."

Emma just blinked at her. "Your what?"

Gracie smiled and looked suddenly more animated than Emma had seen her in a long time. "I want to start a business here on the ranch. Boarding horses, giving riding lessons and mostly, to work on equine therapy."

She stroked her hand along Herman's neck and the older horse leaned into her like a giant puppy looking for more love. Gracie laughed a little and obliged him.

"I totally understand boarding and riding lessons, you'd be great at it. But equine therapy? What made you think of that?"

She'd heard of it, of course. The therapy was designed to help people suffering with everything from PTSD to autism to depression. It could help with physical disabilities as well and was becoming more and more widely accepted.

The familiar scents of hay and horse and weathered wood surrounded Emma like a warm hug as she waited for her sister to speak again.

"I didn't, at first. But when we hired Tom, a year or so ago, he was…on edge a lot."

Emma knew she was talking about Tom Hatton. About forty, with short hair and sad brown eyes. He was quiet, kept to himself, but from what she'd seen, he was a hard worker.

"He's a veteran and he really needed the job. He hadn't done much ranch work, but Dad hired him anyway, because he could see Tom was in a bad way and—"

"Dad's a softy."

Gracie grinned. Sisters, sharing family truths, and it felt good to Emma.

"That he is," Gracie said. "Anyway, over the next few months, as Tom spent time around the horses, grooming and caring for them and learning to ride, he sort of…unwound, you know?"

Emma understood that completely. Horses were soothing to the soul. Just being around them could remind you to pause and enjoy the moment. "Not surprising at all."

"Exactly!"

In her obvious excitement, Gracie had evidently forgotten about any lingering anger she had for her sister and Emma was grateful for it.

"So the horses healed Tom and you figured you could do it for other people, too?"

"Basically." Gracie leaned her forearms on Herman's broad back. "I've studied up on the theories and taken classes at the community college. And Madison Peters, the local vet, is helping me get it started."

"Well, that's really nice of her."

"Yeah." Gracie stiffened a little, then went on. "She's helped me find old or abandoned horses. I've got five now, ready for riding lessons in the spring and Herman here will be the star of the therapy clients." Gracie stroked his neck again. "He was left tied to a fence in the middle of a field outside of town. No one knew where he was from or who had left him, so I went and got him.

"I think Herman and the others are so grateful to be loved and have a home again, that they're eager to be with people."

Emma could never understand how anyone could walk away from the animals who relied on them and she was glad that Herman had found a home with Gracie, who would always care for him.

"I've got two horses that we're boarding right now, too," Gracie said. "So that's good for income, but I'll want to expand and that means adding onto the stable or maybe just building another one."

"Big plans," Emma mused, happy that her sister had found something she was excited about. Something she wanted to do with her life. And Emma was grateful that Gracie wouldn't go through what she had. Working for yourself had to be better than having your life in someone else's hands.

"I know, but I think I can make it work. Dad's all for it and Madison thinks it's a great idea."

"No reason you can't," Emma said with enthusiasm. "It's perfect, Gracie. You're terrific with horses and with people. You were made for this."

"Really?" Gracie looked at her, and it was clear she wanted to believe Emma.

"Really." For the first time since returning to Montana, Emma felt as if there was a chance to win back her sister. To have the kind of relationship they used to have. "I'll support you any way I can. If you need help, just tell me and I'm there."

"Thanks, Emma."

The more she considered it, the better the idea sounded. Gracie had always had a gift with animals. Plus, she was warm and friendly, and was great with kids, too. Which was a good thing because there would always be children wanting to learn to ride.

But as much as she was happy for her sister, Emma was able to look down the road and see a few speed bumps. "How big a stable are you thinking of building?"

"I'd like to have ten horses for lessons and the therapy sessions, and this stable can only hold five, plus the ranch's working horses." She looked at Emma and said, "So the new stable would have to be big enough for the therapy horses, and for boarders. I'd like to use this stable for the ranch animals and keep my business horses separate where I can."

She could actually see it in her mind's eye. "You're right. You'll need a new stable. A big one, with room to grow. You could build it just on the other side of the yard. Separate, but still close to the corral…"

"That's what I was thinking," her sister said, smiling.

Emma loved hearing how sure of herself Gracie sounded and wanted to do everything she could to help. Not only because this was the first time they'd actually "connected" since Emma came home, but because she loved her sister and wanted her happy.

"But it all sounds expensive, right? Have you already gone to the bank to set up a loan?"

Boom. Gracie's features went blank instantly and Emma knew that somehow she'd lost her.

"Not necessary."

"You've already got the money?" Emma asked. "How?" If she'd taken another mortgage out on the house, then Emma wanted to know about it. If she'd gotten the money somewhere else, Emma *really* wanted to know about it.

"I handled it, okay?" Gracie finished grooming Herman and set the comb down on the shelf alongside the door. "This is going to be my business, Emma, and I know what needs to be done. Just like I've handled everything else for the last five years."

Emma's heart sank a little. "Really? We're back to being enemies again?"

"I'm not your enemy, Emma," Gracie said. "But I'm not a kid anymore, either. I can take care of this by myself."

"Damn it, Gracie, stop shutting me out."

But her little sister just shook her head. "Thanks for helping with Herman. I'll see you up at the house later."

When she was alone again, Emma wondered if she'd ever feel as if she'd really come home. It was as if she was still an outsider. A stranger in the place where she'd grown up. Every time she took a step into the circle of family and friends and lovers, that circle narrowed and she found herself still shut out. She'd felt much the same in Hollywood—but here, the pain of it was much sharper because these were her people. This was her place. She needed to be a part of it all again.

Her past was here and this was where she wanted to build a future. But the present was filled with pot-holes and mistrust that she hadn't figured out how to conquer yet.

When Caden's truck pulled into the ranch yard late that afternoon, Emma's heart gave a solid jolt. Her skin buzzed and every one of her nerve endings bristled. She walked out of the house to meet him and her mouth went dry as he climbed out of the truck and settled his hat on his head.

He looked across at her and their gazes clashed with all the heat and need and passion they'd shared during the storm. God, she'd missed him. One day away from him had her burning to hold him, to feel his arms come around her. She wanted his kiss, his touch, and knowing that she couldn't have any of it right now was the only thing that kept her from hur-rying over to him.

Instead, she leaned against a porch post and watched him. "This is a nice surprise. What's up?"

He came around the front of the truck, and everything about him screamed cowboy, badass, *dream lover*.

"Thought I'd come over to meet your...daughter."

Emma threw a quick glance behind her at the house, making sure her father wasn't overhearing the hesitation in Caden's voice. Frowning a little, she waited until he was close enough that she could keep her voice low when she spoke. "Dad doesn't know. Neither does Gracie. You're the only one I've told."

His expression clearly said her he didn't think much of that. "Why, Emma? They're your family. You don't trust them?"

"Of course I do," she whispered, still casting a worried glance at the house behind her. Yes, she felt terrible, keeping this secret from them. But sometimes, hiding the truth was the only way to protect someone you loved. In this case, both Molly and her father.

Then meeting his gaze again, she said, "But Dad's doing so well now, I don't want to throw him back into a decline when he finds out the granddaughter he loves so much isn't really his. How can I tell him?" She straightened up, and shot a look at the stables, where the vet's van was parked. Madison and Gracie were inside, dealing with the horses and Emma hoped they stayed there.

"As for Gracie, well, we haven't exactly been chatty since I came home," she pointed out with a sense of grief over what she'd lost. "Except for earlier today when we managed to actually talk without swiping at each other for like ten minutes, she can hardly stand to be in the same room with me. So pardon me for not catching her arm in the hall and confessing everything."

Caden shook his head and scowled at her. "Em, you're making this harder than it has to be."

"Am I?" she countered. Nerves rattled around in her stomach and she slapped one hand to her belly to try to quiet them. It didn't work. "I don't have legal custody of Molly. All I have is a letter from her mother asking me to take her. I can't tell my family because I don't want to include them in what I've already done by taking Molly.

"Plus, I can't risk someone finding out she isn't mine because what if *they* say something and then that spreads until finally I have Sheriff Eagle dropping by to handcuff me and hand the baby over to social services?"

His eyes widened. "I don't know whether to be impressed or horrified by how your brain works. How the hell do you build up an entire scenario in your head? You don't know any of that would happen."

"I don't know it wouldn't, either," she told him. "I brought Molly here to keep her *safe*."

He yanked his hat off, stabbed his fingers through that thick, beautiful black hair of his, then jammed his hat back on. Narrowing his gaze on her, he said,

"That letter's not enough for you to keep her safe. You know that, right?"

"Thank you, Mr. Obvious. Yes, I know. But it's all I have."

"All right." Caden sighed, looked into the distance for a long second or two, then shifted his gaze back to her. "Here's what we're going to do. I'll take you into Kalispell. We'll talk to my lawyer."

"A *lawyer*?" Panicked at the thought, Emma tried to sift through the dozens of thoughts that sprung into her mind. "I'm trying to hide and you want to take me to a lawyer? Doesn't he have to tell someone? I mean, officer of the court and all that?"

"Confidentiality," Caden reminded her.

Okay, her fear dropped a notch or two. "Right, right."

"I trust Max, Em. I've known him for years. He can give us an idea of what to do from here."

"Us?"

"You," he corrected and Emma was sorry to hear it. For a second there, she'd thought they were a team. "It all boils down to this. Do you trust me, Em?"

That was an easy question to answer. She looked into his eyes and saw the steady, strong man she'd always known. She saw her lover. The man who made her hunger like no one else ever had. His eyes were steady, cool and fixed on hers. Of course she trusted Caden. So she'd trust his lawyer, too. She'd accept his help and be grateful for it.

"Yes, Caden. I do trust you," she said, taking a deep breath of the crisp, cold air. "When do we go?"

"Tomorrow. No point in putting it off, is there?"

"No," Emma said, fighting a fresh tide of fear washing through her, "I guess not. So you want to come in and meet Molly?"

"In a minute." Caden climbed the steps until he was on the porch with her, then he pulled her up close. So close, his belt buckle dug into her middle and the hard, thick proof of his passion pressed against her belly, quickening so many new fires inside her, she could hardly breathe.

Looking into her eyes, he said, "Damn it, Emma, I missed you last night. I didn't want to, but damned if I didn't."

Her heartbeat actually *fluttered*. She hadn't known it could do that. "Oh boy, I missed you, too."

One corner of his mouth lifted and his eyes burned with the heat that could scorch her in seconds. "Good to know." Then he bent his head to kiss her and everything that wasn't Caden drained right out of her mind.

For seconds, minutes, hours? Her mouth tangled with his, their tongues entwined, their breath moving from one to the other and back again. Emma felt herself melting into him and somehow, her mind woke up as she half wondered how she had ever managed to leave him. He was in her heart, her soul. He was so much a part of her that without him, she'd never really felt whole the entire time she was gone.

And Emma knew, with everything in her, that if he wasn't with her, she'd spend the rest of her life with a gaping hole inside. When he finally lifted his head and stared down at her, Emma could only stare back, lost in those cool, blue eyes.

"Well, this is fun. Hi, Caden."

Emma jolted, but he didn't let her go. Just turned his head and said, "Hi, Gracie. Madison."

Blinking hard and fighting for a few remaining brain cells to fire, Emma shifted a glance to her sister and the grinning redhead standing beside her.

"Hi, Caden," she said, then stuck out her right hand. "And you're Emma. Nice to meet you. I've heard a lot about you."

"I'll bet," Emma said, shaking her hand and sparing her sister a quick look.

Gracie shrugged. "Are you two going to stay out here and grope each other or are you coming inside? I'm putting some fresh coffee on."

"Sold," Caden said and when Emma would have moved away from him, he kept one arm around her shoulders, pinning her to his side.

All of them went into the house and while Gracie and Madison headed for the kitchen, Emma and Caden followed the sound of Molly's excited squeal to the great room.

Frank was on the floor, making mooing sounds

and Molly was braced against a pile of pillows, clapping her hands in delight.

"Well, hello, Frank."

Emma laughed as her father looked up. "Hey, Caden, good to see you. Emma, our girl here about said 'cow' a minute ago."

Emma laughed. "Dad, she's not going to talk at five months."

"Can if she wants to. This baby girl is a smart one."

"Is she?" Caden walked over, crouched beside Frank and let the baby give him a thorough inspection. When she finally gave him a toothless grin and babbled a stream of sounds, Caden laughed and Emma's heart stopped.

He reached out, picked her up, and Molly patted his cheeks. "Well, you're a beauty, aren't you?"

Caden shot a look at Emma and just like that, everything in her dissolved into a puddle of goo. What was it about seeing a strong, sexy man being kind and gentle with a baby? It plucked every heartstring and tightened every nerve until her body felt like it was burning up. Her gaze met Caden's and what she saw there fired up her hormones and sent them into a wild dance of anticipation.

This was her cowboy, Emma told herself. And she would never give him up again.

Nine

"Well?" Dorian glared at his assistant— *What* was his name? "What have you got?"

The younger man swallowed hard, looked down at his notes, then spoke quickly, words tumbling over each other. "The investigator made it out of the airport last night finally."

"I didn't ask you for his travel plans, did I?" Dorian felt his temper inching higher and higher. "What did he find?"

Tim—that was his name—Tim, cleared his throat nervously, walked to the desk and timidly set down a sheet of paper. Dorian glanced at it.

"He's got her address, phone number, email. She lives in some tiny town near Kalispell."

Dorian scanned the paper, hardly listening.

But Tim kept talking. "Her family has a small ranch, nothing special. Her father's been in a bad way for a while and her sister's been running the place—"

Finally, Dorian lifted his head and speared little Tim with an icy glare. "What makes you think I care about any of that? I only worry about backstories in my movies. All I need is the information. I've got it now, so get out."

"Yes, sir." Tim turned and scuttled across the room and out the door, shutting it quietly after him.

Dorian's temper was developing a life of its own. He heard his own thundering heartbeat in his ears and could actually *feel* his blood pressure rising. He had about five days before the shit hit the proverbial fan. So this woman…he checked again. Emma Williams. Had better do exactly what he told her to do.

"Well, I like her."

Gracie laughed shortly. "Of course you like Emma, Mad. You like everybody."

"I try to, yes." Madison shrugged and leaned against the wall by the front door. "Why live your life grumpy?"

"Is that a clever way of telling me I'm crabby?"

"I said grumpy."

Gracie nodded. "A fine distinction."

"It is," Madison said with a smile as she straightened up. "And actually, you were pretty nice to

Emma tonight at dinner. Oh, and thank your dad for me. That spaghetti was terrific."

Gracie smiled, too. "His specialty." She glanced toward the great room. "Now that Caden's gone home and the baby's asleep, he's probably nodding off in his chair."

"Sounds good to me," Madison said, stifling a yawn. "I've been up since three when the Porter's dog went into early labor."

"Lots of baby news around here," Gracie muttered.

"And speaking of babies, Molly is adorable." Madison grabbed Gracie's hand and squeezed. "I saw you with her. You're crazy about that little girl."

Sighing, Gracie thought it was just a shame sometimes how easily Madison could read her. There was simply no point in trying to hide things from the woman. "Okay, yes. She's a cutie and yes, I'm nuts about her. Happy?"

Madison laughed, then clapped one hand over her mouth to quiet the sound. "Sorry. Don't want to wake your dad. But yes, I'm not *un*happy. Now, I'm going home to give you and Emma a chance to talk."

"We already did."

"And yet," Madison pointed out, "there's still so much to say."

Gracie shook her head in amazement. "You're really pushy sometimes, did anyone ever tell you that?"

"Only you," she said, then reached out to give

her a hug. "I'll call you tomorrow. Maybe you could come to my place for dinner."

"That sounds great." Gracie opened the front door for her. "Be careful, the roads can be icy."

"Yes, Mom." Madison's laughter trailed after her as she hurried out to her truck.

Gracie stood in the doorway until Madison was on her way, headed down the drive. Then she locked up, and threw a quick look at her dad, asleep in his chair with an open book on his lap and his glasses sliding down the end of his nose. A wave of love for him crashed over her along with that niggling worry she couldn't shake. What would he say if he knew her secret? What would he think of her? What would it change?

She did as she always did, buried those fears deep and tucked them away behind the secret she protected. Taking a deep breath, she walked down the hall to the kitchen because a cup of hot tea sounded perfect. When she entered the big square room, though, she stopped dead. Emma was sitting at the table, scrolling on her phone. She looked up when Gracie came in.

"Hey. I like your friend Madison."

Whether she told herself it didn't matter or not, Gracie was glad to hear that. Lips curving, she admitted, "Mad just said the same thing about you." Picking up the teakettle, she grudgingly offered, "I'm making myself some tea. You want some?"

"Thanks, Gracie. Yeah, I would." Emma sat back in her chair and watched her move around the kitchen.

Familiar tasks freed up your mind for other things, Gracie told herself. Which meant she could think about her sister. She'd really missed Emma all the time she was gone. And she'd been so busy letting her hurt feelings and anger drag her around for the past several days, she hadn't really taken the time to admit that it was good to have her home.

Muffling a groan, Gracie rolled her eyes and thought it was really *frustrating* to have to admit that Mad had been right. Again.

"Oh, my God. No."

Heart suddenly racing, Gracie spun around. Emma's voice was horrified and when she looked at her sister, Gracie could see real fear stamped on her features. "What's wrong, Em? What happened?"

She didn't speak. She just stared at her phone, eyes wide, mouth open as if waiting for a shriek to slip out. A sheen of tears glimmered in her eyes. Gracie'd never seen her big sister like this and she didn't like it.

"Emma." Gracie hurried over to her. "What is it?"

Emma looked at her. "Oh God, Gracie, I don't know what to do."

Gracie dragged a chair out and plopped down, then bracing her forearms on her thighs, she leaned toward her big sister. "You're scaring me."

"I'm scared, too." Emma pulled in a long, shuddering breath and twin tears streaked along her cheeks unheeded.

"Talk to me, Em. Tell me what's going on."

Shaking her head, she handed over her phone. "Here. Just read this. Then I'll explain."

Ms. Williams. You will return my daughter to me or you will be charged with kidnapping. I expect to hear from you immediately. Dorian Baxter

Stunned, shaken and mostly confused, Gracie looked at her sister. "His daughter? Kidnapping? What the hell, Em? Who's Dorian Baxter?"

"Molly's father," Emma blurted, snatching the phone from Gracie and turning it off, as if that could make the email disappear.

"You kidnapped Molly?" If she had said she was a notorious bank robber with a château in France as a safe house, Gracie wouldn't have been more surprised.

"No, of course not," Emma said, shaking her head. "I mean, not really. Legally maybe, but not— Oh, God. What am I going to do?"

Gracie didn't know what to think.

The fear on Emma's face was real, though, and it was contagious, because Gracie's stomach started spinning in sympathy. "Tell me what's happening and maybe we can figure it out."

Panic shining in her eyes, Emma nodded and

reached for her hand. Holding on, she said, "Okay, I'll tell you, but you can't let Dad know. I couldn't bear it if this whole thing made him sick again and—"

So she wasn't the only one with secrets, Gracie thought. Nor the only one worried about upsetting their father. Strangely enough, that knowledge made her feel closer to her sister. "Agreed. Just talk."

Emma did. Gracie sat quietly—it wasn't easy because there were plenty of times she wanted to curse and a few times she wanted to apologize for giving Emma such a hard time since she came home. Her heart hurt for her sister and for Molly and for the baby's mother. But she didn't say a word, just listened. The more she heard, the worse it got. Emma's grip on her hand tightened and Gracie squeezed back in solidarity.

When Emma finally finished talking and silence dropped down on the kitchen, Gracie was as scared as Emma. "I don't even know what to say. This is all—"

"A mess?" Emma asked. "Yeah, I know." Jumping up from her chair, she stared out the window at the darkness beyond. Her reflection stared back into the room and Gracie's gaze met Emma's mirrored eyes.

"He doesn't even really want her, does he?"

"Of course not," Emma said, biting her lip. "I don't know why he's doing this. He didn't give a damn about Terry or Molly, so what's changed?"

She whirled around to look at Gracie. "Nope, doesn't matter what changed. I won't do it. I don't care what happens to me, I'm not giving Molly to that man. I just won't."

"Damn straight you won't."

Emma and Gracie both jolted and turned around to face their father, standing in the doorway. Frank Williams was furious and Gracie couldn't remember the last time she'd seen him with his temper boiling. His usually placid features were a thunderstorm and his eyes were flashing. Under the overhead light, his gray hair was rumpled from his nap, but his features were set like an ancient warrior about to go into battle.

"Dad," Emma said quickly, "I never meant to hurt you. I mean, I know you thought she was your granddaughter, but I didn't know how to tell you the truth and—"

"Dad, maybe you should sit down," Gracie interrupted Emma.

"I don't need to sit down," he said, biting off every word.

Gracie blinked and threw a quick look at her sister. She looked as confused and surprised as Gracie felt.

But Frank was still talking so they both paid attention. "As for Molly, she *is* my granddaughter and I'll fight anyone who says different."

Gracie looked at Emma again and saw tears coursing down her sister's face. Her own heart turned over in sympathy. Gracie had assumed Emma's life was perfect, unlike her own. Instead, her sister had been worrying in silence, hugging her secrets close, just as Gracie was. And rather than seeing past her own anger long enough to actually talk to Emma, Gracie had kept them at odds when they might have been helping each other. If she could have kicked her own ass, she would have.

But right now, she had other worries. "Dad? Are you okay?"

He looked at Gracie. "Stop watching me like you're waiting for me to keel over. I feel fine. I'm just mad as hell is all."

"Okay…" He did have fire in his eyes and his shoulders were squared, his spine ramrod straight.

"I wanted to tell you before, Dad," Emma was saying, "I just didn't know how."

"Doesn't matter," he ground out and walked to her. Pulling her in for a hug, he kissed the top of Emma's head and said, "That baby belongs with us. I won't see her go to a father who doesn't deserve her. Especially not to a man like that one. Damned if I will."

"But she's not my daughter." Emma's voice broke. "I don't know what we can do."

Frank looked from one to the other of his daughters and said, "She may not be your daughter, but she's our family. We love her and when it all boils down, love is the only thing that matters."

Gracie's heart lifted and tears stung her eyes as she moved across the kitchen to join the group hug. This was what she'd needed to hear all along. This was what she needed to believe. She should have trusted that her father would be the man to see clearly right down to the heart of the matter.

"Caden's taking me to Kalispell tomorrow to talk to his lawyer."

"That's a good idea," Frank said.

"It is good," Gracie chimed in, looking into Emma's eyes to reassure her. "Max will know what to do."

"That's right, he will. And if he for some reason can't come up with a plan, don't you two worry," Frank said softly, holding them both. "We'll figure this out. Together."

The next morning, Emma was at Caden's ranch just after dawn. She hadn't been able to sleep and after trying most of the night, she'd given up and headed to the only man who could, hopefully, untie the knots in her stomach.

They'd be meeting with his lawyer in a few hours and Emma's nerves were strung so tight, it was a wonder her body wasn't throwing off sparks.

Caden opened the door and she only stared at him for a long minute. His chest was bare, his jeans on but unbuttoned and his hair was still damp from his shower. Instantly, her mouth went dry and heat rushed through her body.

"Emma, what're you doing here? I was going to pick you up in a couple hours."

"Couldn't sleep," she admitted and slipped past him into the house. She dropped her black shoulder bag on the entry table, then turned to face him. "I'm all tangled up inside, Caden."

He closed the door, then leaned back against it, folding his arms across his chest. He looked her up and down slowly and his gaze felt as hot as a touch. Straightening up, he moved to her, laid both hands on her shoulders and she felt the fire of him slide deep within her.

"You're smart, beautiful and brave," he said softly. "And Max is a damn good lawyer. So stop worrying."

"I can't," she said. "My mind keeps spinning and—"

He grinned. "Then let's give it something else to think about." He kissed her and instantly, Emma's mind emptied.

His mouth claimed hers, his tongue twisting with hers, his breath sighing into her lungs. She slid her hands up and down his bare back, her fingernails scraping his skin. He dropped his hands to her butt and squeezed, pulling her in so tight, she felt his erection pressing against her.

Anticipation rolled through her. Excitement. Eagerness. She wanted him. This was why she'd had to come to him. He was the only man in the world who could turn her fears and nerves into blistering hot desire.

"Jacket off," he muttered when he tore his mouth free.

"Okay." She slid it off and let it drop to the floor.

"And the shirt," he ordered. "Take it off, but be sure to wear it a lot after today. I like it."

Emma tipped her head to one side. "You know I don't take orders, right?"

One corner of his mouth lifted. "You do today."

He wasn't wrong. There wasn't a woman alive who could stand in front of a half-naked Caden and say "no."

She smiled even as her breath came faster, harder. The red, scoop neck, long-sleeved shirt was alongside her jacket in seconds.

"Now the boots. And the slacks." He watched her strip right there in the foyer and his eyes gleamed with a dark heat that fired everything inside her.

Lastly, she stepped out of the black lace panties that had gotten a low whistle from Caden, and she was naked in moments. Then she was in his arms and while her mind was quiet, her body was burning.

He grabbed her, lifted her and swung around to plant her back against the closed door. The wood panel was cold against her skin, but couldn't dampen the fires licking at her bones, her blood, her soul.

Emma hooked her legs around his hips and watched as he freed himself from his jeans. She reached down to curl her fingers around the thick length of him and watched his eyes glaze over. Then he growled and in an instant, he was inside her, filling her. She tipped her head back against the door and stared at the ceiling as he drove her past sanity into a world that revolved only around the two of them.

Again and again, he took her, pushing her higher, faster, than ever before. She lowered her gaze to meet his and saw an all-encompassing desire to match her own. His hunger was etched on his face and seeing it, fed hers.

Fast. So fast. She had been primed for this before she arrived and now, the payoff was almost on her. She felt a climax coming and welcomed it. Rushed to meet it. His big, strong hands cupped her butt, supporting her while he pushed into her depths with desperation. Together, they raced toward that end that was always more of a beginning for them. An orgasm didn't finish things between them, it only set them up for the next one. And Emma knew she would never have him enough. Never lose this magic that happened only when he was inside her.

"Stop thinking, Em," he ordered. "Feel me. Feel me inside you and come. Let go and come."

"I am," she said, as splintering sensations opened

up deep within her. She locked her gaze with his. "Right now."

And her body exploded. She called out his name helplessly as wave after wave of satisfaction flooded her system. His gaze held hers and she couldn't have looked away even if she'd wanted to. Instead, she watched as his body joined hers, as her name erupted from his lips. As his eyes burned into hers.

When the trembling stopped, she dropped her head to his shoulder. "Well, you did it. I'm not worried anymore."

He gave a short bark of laughter. "Then my work here is done."

She looked him in the eye. "Oh no, it's not."

"Good to know," he answered and bent his head to give her a quick kiss.

Then something occurred to her and she blurted out, "We didn't use a condom."

Caden shrugged. "If something happens, we'll deal with it then."

A tiny flicker of hope for a future flared to life in her heart. If he wasn't worried by a pregnancy scare, then he was thinking beyond the moment.

Lifting her off him, he looked down at her. "I think we could both use another shower."

Her legs were still trembling, but she nodded, because she had a vision of shower sex floating through her mind.

"You go on up. I'll get your stuff."

"You're really bossy this morning," she said, a soft smile curving her mouth.

"You complaining?"

"Not today," she said, because really, all she could think about was having him again. Then she turned and started up the stairs. Feeling his gaze on her, Emma deliberately swung her hips and paused halfway up to look over her shoulder at him.

His eyes were on fire. "You trying to tell me something, Em?"

She licked her lips, tossed her hair back and gave an order to him for a change. "You bet. Get moving, cowboy. I want that shower."

He grinned. "Yes, ma'am."

A few hours later, Caden sat next to Emma at his lawyer's office. That email from Dorian Baxter had to be handled legally and Caden knew they had to act fast. If they hadn't had to be here, he never would have left the ranch. Not after having Emma against the door, in the shower and on the bed. The woman stirred him up like no one else.

Even thinking about their morning was enough to stir his blood and make his dick cry for mercy.

Max Finley scanned the letter from Terry that Emma had handed him and when he was finished reading, he looked up and took off his glasses. "This is the only proof of custody you have?"

Emma blindly reached for Caden's hand and he took it, folding his fingers around hers.

"Yes." Emma's voice sounded breathy, vulnerable, and Caden didn't like it. "She left me that note the day she died."

Max leaned back in the burgundy leather chair. "It's not enough. You know that, don't you?"

"Yes, I do," she said softly. "But I couldn't leave Molly with that man. He didn't want her. I can't imagine why he's trying to get her now."

Caden hated hearing that uncertainty and fear in Emma's voice. He owed this Dorian Baxter a world of hurt for causing it.

"Probably someone found out about the baby," Caden said. "Maybe they're hoping to make him look bad and he's trying to head that off at the pass."

"Could be," Max mused, then his gaze fixed on Emma again. "Do you have any evidence of what you say he did to your roommate? Any proof at all of his character?"

"Or lack thereof," Caden muttered. It would almost be worth a flight to Hollywood if he could plant his fist in the man's face.

Max nodded at him.

But Emma said, "No. No proof. But it's an open secret in Hollywood. People know what he's like, it's just that no one talks about it."

"Again, it's simply not enough."

"Look, Max," Caden said gruffly, "what Emma's

done was to protect that baby. You have to admire that. God knows I do."

From the corner of his eye, he saw Emma's surprise. He couldn't blame her for that. Over the last week or so, they'd been closer than ever before and at the same time, as distant as the earth from the moon. Having her here again tangled Caden up in so many knots, he couldn't count them all. Hours ago, she'd been naked in his bed and God knew he still wanted her. Still loved her. But how the hell was he supposed to trust her to stay?

She'd left him to chase a dream and run home when that dream crashed down around her. But if they went forward from here, didn't that make Caden her second choice? How could he live with that? How could he spend the rest of his life wondering if she'd always be looking for more than they had together?

He didn't know where the hell they went from here, but Caden would do all he could to help her protect her friend's baby. Because Caden hated men who took advantage of women. He'd do whatever he could to keep that child away from a man who drove her mother to suicide. And because he'd do anything for Emma—anything but trust her.

"Listen, Max," he said, "Baxter doesn't know what Emma might have. For all he knows, she's got Terry's diary, spelling out everything."

"I think I see where you're going," Max said, and a slow smile spread across his face. "We send an email—

followed up by a very official registered letter—telling him to back off or our evidence will go public."

"Exactly," Caden said, nodding. "In the current atmosphere—especially in Hollywood—his career would be over."

"You really think it'll work?" Emma asked.

He looked her in the eye. "I do. Baxter won't want to test us. He has too much to lose." Then he turned to face his lawyer again. "But on the off chance he won't let this go, I want you to do something for me."

Max smiled again. This is why he was Caden's lawyer. They'd been friends for years and were usually on the same page about most things.

"Let me guess," Max mused. "You want me to hire an investigator in LA. Do some quick digging."

"Always said you were a smart guy," Caden said. "Hire as many investigators as you think we need. Offer bonuses if they come up with something fast that we can use against this guy."

"Caden… I can't pay for that," Emma protested.

"I didn't ask you to." Caden caught her gaze and held it. "You can be hardheaded about something else, okay? Let this one go."

She thought about it for a minute and he knew her pride had to be dented. But finally, she nodded. "Okay. For Molly. And thanks."

"I know some people in LA," Max said. "I'll make some calls and get this moving."

"Thanks, Max. Knew I could count on you."

* * *

Emma was grateful for Caden's help. Without him doing all of this, she didn't know what she would have done. The thought of giving the baby over to Dorian Baxter was enough to give a statue cold chills. The only other thing she could have done was take the baby and run—and God knew how that would have ended.

At Tucker's, a steak house just outside Kalispell, Emma looked across the table at him. He was dressed all in black but for the crisp white dress shirt beneath his jacket. His black hat and gleaming black boots only added to the picture of professional, gorgeous and just that delicious touch of wicked that she loved.

She'd seen that wicked side of him a few hours ago. And just remembering what they'd done sent a thrill up her spine and settled an ache between her thighs. How could she want him so much? And what would she do if he pulled back from her? If he never believed that she was home to stay?

"Thank you, Caden," she said when the waiter left after taking their order.

"For lunch? Not a problem."

"Not for lunch. For what you're doing for me and Molly."

He sipped at his beer, then set it down on the white-cloth-covered table. He was quiet, thoughtful and for a few seconds, Emma held her breath.

"I don't like men who use power against people," he said. "And I really don't like them using it against *you*."

A flush of warmth raced through her and her heart filled with hope again. Hope that there was a future for them.

Coming here, to Tucker's was a good sign, too. This used to be "their" place. The restaurant had been in the same spot for fifty years. There was a stone hearth, with a roaring fire sending waves of heat across the room. Dozens of heavy wooden tables, draped with midnight blue cloths were crowded with laughing, talking people and the restaurant served the best steaks in Montana.

"Do you think it'll work? Bluffing Dorian?"

"I think so." He shrugged and didn't look the least bit worried. "If it doesn't, Max will get a backup plan in place."

Something suddenly occurred to her and Emma said softly, "Speaking of plans, Gracie told me what she's going to build at the ranch."

"Did she? Well, good."

"She said she already had the money for the project," Emma added. "You loaned it to her, didn't you?"

His eyes flashed and his lips twisted into a frown. "Yeah, I did. It's a good idea and Gracie will be great at it. She's smart and steady and she works hard. So if you're thinking of giving me grief over it—"

"Thank you."

He stopped midsentence and stared at her. "You

surprise me, Emma. I expected anger from you over this. You haven't been real happy with what close friends Gracie and I are. I wasn't expecting gratitude."

"Well," she said, "I am grateful. For this. For all the help you gave my dad while I was gone. For looking out for my family while I was gone."

"You don't have to thank me," he said tightly.

"I am anyway, so just deal with it."

He laughed shortly. "That's more like the Emma I know."

"Emma?"

She turned in her chair and grinned as Jess Whitehead hurried over to the table. The woman shot Caden a quick smile. "Hi, Caden, good to see you."

"You, too, Jess."

"I'm not going to interrupt—well, not for long anyway," she said with a laugh. "Did Gracie give you my message?"

"What? No," Emma said, curious now. "But with the storm and everything, she probably forgot." At least she hoped that was the reason Gracie hadn't said anything.

"Well, I'll make this quick. Gracie said you're back to stay?"

"I am." She looked at Caden and saw in his eyes that he still didn't believe her on that score.

"That's great. Since you're staying, I've got a job for you."

Curious, she asked, "What kind of job?"

"You know I'm the principal of Cache High, right?"

"I do now. Imagine that. The ditching queen is now the principal." Emma laughed, remembering all the times she and Jess had cut school to go to a movie or shopping, or pretty much for any reason at all.

"Hmm," Jess said, with a wry smile. "Ironic, huh? Anyway, I need a drama teacher and I've already spoken to the superintendent and he said that with your education and real-world experience, you qualify for a provisional teaching certificate…"

"Me? A teacher?" Emma thought the idea was crazy, and yet, something about it really appealed to her. What was the old saying? "Those who can't, teach."

"You'd be great, Emma. Tell you what, come to the school tomorrow, I'll introduce you around and you can think about it." She glanced over her shoulder and waved at her husband at a far table. "I've gotta go. Bill's waiting. I'll see you tomorrow?"

"Um, sure," Emma said hesitantly. "I guess so."

"Great. Good to see you, Caden!" Then she was gone.

He was watching her and she could see questions in his eyes. "What do you think?"

Caden picked up his beer, studied the label for a long minute, then said softly, "I think if you were really planning on staying, you'd have jumped at that job."

She flushed and felt the heat of it rising inside. Would he ever believe her? Trust her? He wanted her. Might even still love her, but he didn't trust her and she had no one to blame for that but herself. "I am staying, Caden."

His gaze fixed on hers. "Then take the job, Emma."

"There's other things to consider, you know," Emma argued, wondering if he would ever stop looking at her with suspicion, mistrust. "There's Molly to look after, and the ranch. Dad and Gracie."

"The ranch and your family survived you being gone for five years. I think they could make it through you having a day job." He set his beer down and leaned in toward her, keeping his voice low enough that no one would overhear him. His gaze held hers as he said flatly, "I think you didn't take it because you weren't sure you'd be here long enough to make it worthwhile. I think you've kept one foot out the door this whole time, Emma."

"You're wrong. I am staying, Caden." Frustrated now, she clamped her mouth shut when the waiter delivered their meals. But once he was gone again, Emma leaned toward Caden and lowered her voice. "After how we spent our morning, how can you not know what you mean to me?"

He leaned in, too. "That was sex, Em. Great sex, but that's all."

"Liar," she countered. "It was more than that and you know it."

He took another sip of his beer. His eyes were cool. Distant. And she wanted the fire back.

"How can I make you believe me?"

"You can't, Emma." He said it offhandedly, but his gaze never wavered. "You walked away once. Why shouldn't I expect you to do it again?"

Then he dismissed the conversation completely, sat back and sliced into his filet mignon. Hurt, frustrated and yes, angry again, Emma looked down at her strip steak and pushed it aside. Her throat was so tight now, she wouldn't have been able to swallow.

Caden suddenly felt further away from her than ever.

Ten

The next day, Emma was back in high school. It still smelled the same. Hormones, hair spray and desperation. What was amazing to her was how much *smaller* everything seemed.

"We've got a growing drama department," Jess was saying and ushered Emma back to the costume and props area behind the stage in the gym. "A big donor in Kalispell gave us a ton of money because his grandson went here and loved being in the plays."

Emma stood in the center of the room and did a slow turn, admiring everything. There were racks and racks of costumes, glass-fronted shelves holding wigs and hats and along one wall were stacks of props and plywood ready to be built into whatever backdrop was needed.

When Emma herself took drama at the high school, they'd had donated old clothes from local families and whatever furniture they could scrounge from local charity shops. Things change, she told herself.

"This is amazing…"

"I know, right?" Jess grinned, grabbed Emma's hand and tugged her along behind her. "The former drama teacher took a job in Miami, so we really need you, Emma. The kids are great and they're so excited to meet you."

She laughed a little. "Why?"

"You've been on TV," Jess said. "You're from Cache and you succeeded in Hollywood!"

Success, she knew, could look like different things to different people. And Emma had to admit that if she'd had a teacher who'd actually worked in television, she'd have been impressed, too. It wasn't until actually *going* to Hollywood herself that she'd found out the truth of the shiny, unreachable goal.

"Come on, I want you to meet a few of the kids."

Nerves rippled inside Emma. If she took this job, it might prove to Caden that she was staying. But should she have to prove herself? Couldn't he take her at her word? Was she going to have to pay penance for years for taking a chance on her dream? In spite of the help he'd offered yesterday, she couldn't help but remember how the day had ended. With mistrust. Suspicion.

But this wasn't only about what was between her and Caden, Emma told herself. Taking this job, she'd be walking a fine line between encouraging the kids to go for what they wanted while at the same time cautioning them about a hard reality. Would they want to hear it?

It had been a while since she'd had to relate to a teenager. But when she stepped out onto the stage where two girls and a boy were waiting for her, Emma immediately felt at home. This school, this very stage, had first awakened her dreams of stardom. Seeing the expression on the faces of these kids, she knew they were feeling the same thing she had so long ago.

"Ms. Williams!" One of the girls, a short brunette, hurried forward. "Mrs. Whitehead says you're the new drama teacher."

"Well—"

"I *loved* you in *Space Port*," the boy said. "The way they wrote you as stupid but you played her as more mysterious than that."

"Thanks," she said, glad someone had noticed that she'd tried to give her airhead character on that series a little more depth.

"And what was it like working with Jacob Hall?" the last girl asked, eyes shining with excitement.

Jacob Hall, the gorgeous star of their short-lived

series, was as empty as he was pretty, but Emma doubted that they wanted to hear *that*.

"He's a very good actor," she said instead, and at least it was the truth.

"You know what?" Jess smiled at Emma. "I'll just leave you here to talk to the kids about drama class and about the play they want to put on next spring."

"Oklahoma!" One of the girls said. "I love the music and we were just talking about set decorations…"

Emma laughed a little as she looked from one animated face to the other. Their enthusiasm was contagious. She remembered when her class had done *Oklahoma!* and Emma had played Ado Annie and except for the fact that she wasn't much of a singer, had had a great time.

The boy said, "My dad said he'd help build whatever we need."

"And my dad said he could provide haystacks and stuff…"

Emma's head was spinning, but she hardly noticed when Jess left. Instead, she was drawn into the stardom dreams again. This time through these kids who had stars in their eyes and hope in their hearts. A part of her wanted to warn them to not give up everything in pursuit of something else. But she also realized that they wouldn't believe her—that was a lesson you had to learn yourself. As she had—chasing a dream had cost her Caden.

She also acknowledged that the chances that any of them would have the kind of career they wanted were tiny. But was that any reason to stop dreaming? To stop reaching for what you wanted?

And maybe, Emma told herself, if she could give them real-world tips and warnings and teach them what they needed to make a real try at it…none of them would be as crushed as she had been.

With the kids talking, planning, peppering her with questions about agents and producers and scripts, Emma smiled and took another step toward being a part of Cache again. And soon, Caden would have to admit that she was here to stay. Then he'd have to deal with what was between them. Because she wouldn't let him ignore it much longer.

"I took the job." Emma stood in the kitchen looking at her father and sister. Molly was sitting in her high chair while Gracie fed her spoonfuls of baby food.

"That's great news," her father said, and stood up to give her one of his famous bear hugs. "And don't you worry about Molly. Gracie and I can watch her during the day while you're at school…"

"We can?" Gracie fed Molly another bite of applesauce.

Emma knew what her sister was thinking and she didn't want to risk the tentative moves they'd made toward fixing their relationship. So she said quickly, "You don't have to. I'll get a babysitter and—"

Her father shot that idea down. "We're not going to have strangers watching our girl, are we, Grace?"

"Oh no," Gracie blurted, standing up. "If Emma needs something, let's just rush to accommodate her! How high would you like me to jump, Emma? Any specific direction you'd like to see?"

"Gracie…" Their father sounded disappointed.

And Emma's heart sank. She and her sister had started coming together and now, it seemed they were back to square one again.

"No, Dad. Emma shows up and the whole world falls at her feet. She's even got her hooks back into Caden!" Shaking her head, Gracie held up both hands and said, "I've got to go check on the horses."

Emma could have let her leave, let the fury between them keep simmering, but she'd finally reached maximum tolerance. She'd tried patience. Tried to be understanding and apologetic and it had gotten her exactly nowhere. They were going to get everything out and settle this, whether Gracie liked it or not.

"Don't worry about your sister—"

Emma looked up at her father. "Would you watch Molly for me?"

"Sure, but—"

"Thanks, Dad." Emma raced out of the house and toward the stable. The air was cold, but Emma's anger kept her warm as she hurried across the yard. She found Gracie outside Herman's stall.

Gracie heard her run into the stable, but she didn't turn to look at her. "I don't want to talk to you," she said.

"Fabulous. Then just listen instead," Emma countered, then led with, "Why are you so bugged that Caden and I are together again? Have your eye on him?"

Gracie whirled around, more surprised than angry. "You're nuts."

"Is that right?"

"Yeah." Gracie slapped her hands onto her hips and faced Emma down. "Caden's my *friend*. He was there for me when you abandoned us. I was twenty when you took off, Emma. What the hell did I know about running this ranch?" She threw her hands up. "What did I know about *anything*? Now you're back and you pick up your life like you were never gone. You've got Caden and Molly and a job and I'm still running in place living a lie!"

Gracie clapped one hand over her mouth, horrified that she'd slipped and hoping that Emma would just let it go. Or maybe, she wouldn't care what she'd meant. Her heart pounding, she turned away from her sister and took a deep breath to ease the wild jitters in her belly.

"Gracie, tell me what's going on. What're you talking about?"

Shaking her head, she looked back at Emma and let out a long sigh. "Nothing. And I'm sorry I got mad. I wasn't even really mad at you, Emma." Looking at the older sister she'd always admired, Gracie could admit to herself at last, that it was because Emma had always gone after what she wanted that she'd looked up to her. Emma fought for what she wanted. While Gracie kept quiet and pretended everything was fine.

"Then why all the venom?" Emma asked. "If it's not my fault, why yell at me?"

"Because it's just not as satisfying to yell at myself," Gracie muttered thickly. "I'm mad at *me*, Em. God, I never thought of myself as a coward, but I so am."

"No, you're not." Emma grabbed her arm and squeezed. "Sweetie, you're one of the strongest women I know."

Gracie choked out a laugh and shook her head. "I wish that was true."

Frustrated, Emma threw both hands in the air. "For heaven's sake, Gracie, just *tell* me what's going on. Maybe I can help."

She couldn't help and Gracie knew it. But the need to talk to her big sister was huge. Ever since Emma had come home, Gracie had wanted to confide in her, but anger and resentment had clouded everything to the point where she felt as if she were wandering around the ranch blindfolded.

Looking at Emma now, seeing the confusion and sympathy in her eyes, helped Gracie decide to just take the plunge. To get everything out in the open. It would be a relief to say it out loud, even if nothing came of it. Even if Emma looked at her differently afterward.

"Okay," she said, steeling herself for whatever might happen next. "I'm not interested in Caden, because I'm already in love." She stuffed her hands into her coat pockets. "I haven't told anyone but Caden..."

There was a long pause, then Emma said, "I'm glad you had him to talk to. But it's great news, Gracie. Why wouldn't you want everyone to know?"

The stable was cold and watery sunlight pouring through the open doors was the only light. They were alone but for the horses in their stalls, and the air was so quiet it seemed made for revelations of secrets. She looked at Emma. "Because I'm afraid how Dad will take it."

"He'd be happy for you," Emma said and Gracie so wished she could believe that.

"I don't know if he would be or not," Gracie admitted. "All I know is it's killing me and it's hurting Mad."

"Madison?" Emma whispered. "The vet?"

"Yes!" She blew out a breath and felt relief course through her like a cool rain on a hot day. God, it was freeing to admit the truth. To feel the freedom of saying that she was in love with a wonderful, talented, kind, funny woman. "I'm in love with Mad. Have been almost from the moment I met her."

Emma just watched her. Didn't say anything, and Gracie's fears rose up inside to grab hold of her throat and squeeze. She was laying everything out and if she lost her sister, she didn't know what she'd do.

A single tear tracked down her cheek before Gracie swiped it away angrily. Lifting her chin, squaring her shoulders, she said, "There. My big secret life. I'm a lesbian, and I didn't know how to tell you or Dad because I was terrified of how you guys would take it."

A couple of seconds ticked past before her sister spoke.

"You idiot." Emma's voice was quiet.

That she hadn't expected. "What?"

Her big sister stepped up to her and wrapped Gracie up in a tight hug. "I called you an idiot. How could you think I would care? Gracie, you're my baby sister. Whoever you love is okay by me. I'll love her, too. As long as she treats you right and doesn't make you cry, because then she'd be in big trouble with me—"

Fresh tears sprung to her eyes and these she didn't bother wiping away. They felt cleansing somehow. She couldn't believe this. Ever since Emma got home, Gracie had worried about what her sister would think. What she might say if she found out the truth. It was a shock to find out she hadn't had to worry at all.

Gracie's throat tightened as Emma stepped back and looked her dead in the eye. "As for Dad? He'd be furious if he knew that you were anxious about this. Dad's not going to care who you love, Gracie. For God's sake, it's the twenty-first century, sweetie."

Her big revelation had fallen flat.

Gracie felt both relieved and a little embarrassed that she'd made this into such a huge deal in her mind. "God, I do feel like an idiot."

"Good, you should." Emma squeezed her hard again, then let her go. "I love you, Gracie, and I want you happy. If Mad does that for you, then I'm really glad you found her."

More tears built up in her eyes, but this time, it was liberation. Happiness. The unbelievable sensation of finally being true to herself. She let out a breath that she felt as though she'd been holding since Madison first moved to town. Longer. It seemed as if all her life, Gracie had been hiding the truth of who she was.

"It's not fair to Madison you know," Emma was saying. "Keeping her a secret."

Guilt pinged inside Gracie as she nodded. All the nights she'd sneaked over to Madison's house for a few stolen hours. The days they spent together, but unable to touch, or hold hands or even give each other a kiss goodbye for fear someone would notice. "I know that. I do. But I was just so scared to say anything—"

"No buts, Gracie," Emma told her. "Didn't Dad just say the other night that *love* is the only thing that really matters? That's all he'll care about. That you're loved."

Was it really that simple? Had she been putting herself and Mad through misery all this time for nothing?

"If you want me to, I'll be there when you tell Dad," Emma said softly.

Gracie looked at her and nodded. "I'd like that. Thanks, Em."

Emma grinned, hugged her again, then said, "Okay, now that you and I are good again, I'm going to tell Caden I've got a job. Maybe then he'll believe that I'm really staying."

"You still love him, don't you?"

"More than anything," Emma answered.

Gracie smiled. "Then *make* him believe."

Caden was saddling up for a ride when Emma strode into the stable, looking like a woman on a mission. She simply took his breath away. That long, curly hair flying out behind her. Tight black jeans, cream-colored sweater and a forest green jacket and scuffed brown boots. Heat pumped through him in a rush. She walked with confidence, always had. She was strong, hardheaded, and if he allowed it, she could bring him to his knees.

But he'd done that once. Given her everything, offered her all he was, all he'd hoped to be, and she'd left him broken. He wouldn't let that happen again no matter how much he loved her and wanted her.

She was smiling when she came to a stop just in front of him and God, what that smile did to her eyes. What it did to *him*. His whole body went tight with tension. His blood simmered in a slow boil and it felt like his skin was electrified. This wasn't going to be easy, he told himself, stepping back from the only woman he'd ever loved. But he refused to risk the kind of pain he'd already survived again.

"Gracie told me her secret."

He nodded, glad for that. Whatever happened—or didn't—between the two of them, Emma and Gracie were sisters and he was pleased they'd finally talked. "Happy to hear it. Worrying over it has been tearing at her for a long time."

"You've been a good friend to her," Emma said. "Thank you for that. Seems you're pretty important to both of the Williams girls."

He tightened the saddle cinch on his horse and forced a short laugh. "You know, I wouldn't have slept with Gracie even if she wasn't a lesbian."

"Is that right?"

He shot her a look and his heart thumped hard

in his chest. "It is. Because you're the one I always wanted."

"I'm right here," she said softly.

And the scent of her was filling him. The urge to take her, hold her, was almost overwhelming, and still, he fought it.

"For how long, Emma?" That was at the bottom of all of this. The one thing he couldn't forget. She'd left once. Why wouldn't she again?

"For good, Caden." She moved in closer, laid one hand on his arm and said, "I took the job at Cache High. I'm teaching drama."

That sounded like a good thing, but jobs could be walked out on if she found something better. He couldn't forget that she'd turned away from the plans they'd made together to find something for herself somewhere else.

"That's good, Em," he said, turning to face her, to meet her eyes. Everything about her called out to him, but he ignored it. "You'll be great at it. But you taking a job's not proof that you're staying. You walked out on your life—me—before."

She sighed and he could read the disappointment in her eyes. "That was different, Caden," she said. "I was a kid. I'd never been out of Montana and suddenly we were talking about getting married and having babies and—"

"And you ran," he finished for her, feeling the fresh sting of that betrayal all over again. She'd crushed him once. He wouldn't allow it to happen again.

"I had to go," she argued. "But I came back, too."

"Because California didn't work out. If it had, you'd still be there, wouldn't you?"

"No," she said, shaking her head. "California wasn't my place. I didn't belong, Caden. Everything about it felt wrong to me. I belong here. With you."

God, he wished he could believe her.

She must have read his features accurately because she asked, "How do I convince you?"

"Hell if I know," he said.

"I love you, Caden."

He closed his eyes briefly and savored those words. He'd never thought to hear her say it again and it was like having fresh air breathed into starving lungs. But he couldn't bring himself to trust it. Maybe it was something inside him that couldn't bend. If that were true, then he didn't know how to change it—or even if he should try.

"I love you, too, Em," he said and her eyes brightened before he qualified that statement with, "But I don't trust you."

She winced and he hated to see it. Hated to know that he'd caused it. But she had to know. Love wasn't always enough.

"I don't know how to fix that," she admitted. "How to convince you."

"I don't think you can. You already told me your-self that if you had to, you'd take Molly and run."

She spun around, took two steps away from him, then came right back. "*You* changed that. You have your lawyer working on it for me."

He nodded. Caden had had a lot of time to think since that trip into Kalispell. And he'd come to one solid conclusion. Loving, wanting, even needing wasn't enough. He had to know that he could be-lieve in Emma. Trust that she'd be there, not going off looking for some other "dream" that looked bet-ter than real life.

"And if Max can't solve this? Then what?"

"I—don't know," she admitted. "I'll have to find another way to fight Dorian Baxter. And I will fight."

"And if you lose, you grab Molly and disappear?"

She didn't say anything and Caden knew she didn't have to. Shaking his head, he said quietly, "See? Emma, I admire you for your determination to save that baby. And I'll do whatever I can to help you. But I won't risk believing in you again only to watch you disappear."

"Caden—"

He kissed her deeply, savoring the moment, relish-ing the feel of her body leaning into his, then lifted his head, her taste swimming through his mind. "I'll help, Em. Any way I can. And I'll always love you. But I won't be with you."

She took a step back and looked so shocked and hurt that it tore at him. "Just like that? It's done?"

"Has to be," he said and it cost him. Caden wanted nothing more than to hold on to her, to skim his hands up and down her body, to slide into her heat and lose himself in her.

But it wouldn't change anything. Fix anything. He had to get used to living without her.

"Caden, are you really going to walk away from me?"

"I'm going to make a hell of a good attempt at it." He grabbed his hat off his head, shoved one hand through his hair and said, "Damn it, Emma, when I asked what you'd do if Max couldn't help, you should have said you'd come to me. That you'd trust *me* enough to help you stand against that bastard."

"But your first instinct is still to leave. To go somewhere else. On your own."

When she would have argued, Caden shook his head firmly. "You don't see it. The dreams we'd build together are bigger than anything we could do alone."

"I *am* trusting you, Caden," she argued and he could see in her eyes she believed that.

"Until you can't," he said tightly. "I'm not going to watch you leave again, Em, looking for something else. Something different. Or better. I need you to believe in *us*, not just yourself."

"I've been on my own for five years, Caden," she reminded him. "That's a hard habit to break."

"Maybe it is. But it was your choice, Em. You left. You stayed away even when you yourself said you should have come home sooner."

"Caden—"

Shaking his head, Caden looked at the woman he loved and tried to take a hard step back. "Home was your second choice, Em. If you had a shot at stardom again, you'd be gone again. Until you're really *here*, there's nothing for us."

Without another word, he shoved his foot in the stirrup, swung aboard his horse and rode out of the stable, leaving her alone in the shadows.

Eleven

A few hours later, Emma was back home, watching Gracie and Madison laughing together. Gracie's "secret" hadn't been as secret as she'd thought. When her little sister had finally taken the plunge and talked to their father, Frank had said only, "Hell, I know that."

After Gracie's surprise wore off, Frank had kissed his youngest daughter and sent her off to bring Madison home for dinner.

Now, Emma had to wonder how she could have missed how her sister and Madison looked at each other. She saw the same gleam of love in Gracie's eyes that shone for Caden in her own.

Now that their secret was out, they were holding

hands, finishing each other's sentences and looking so damn happy, they were both beaming.

They talked about their plans for the new stable and Gracie's business, and Madison had some great ideas. The two of them were going to make a terrific team. And, Emma felt like a ghost at a wedding. Happiness bubbled all around her, but she couldn't catch any of it for herself. She kept remembering Caden riding away, leaving her alone. And she was forced to realize that was how he must have felt when she'd turned away from him.

God, she hadn't known. Hadn't realized what she was sacrificing for the chance at a nebulous dream. Yes, if she hadn't tried, she might have regretted it all her life. But trying and failing had cost her both the dream and Caden.

Losing that dream was hard, but losing Caden was unbearable. Emma simply could not imagine a life without him in it.

"You know," Frank said idly, "Madison, there's no reason you can't move in here with us."

"What?" She looked from Frank to Gracie and back again. "Really?"

"Sure. No reason for you to be driving in and out of here at all hours. Winter's coming and the road to town is going to get bad. Besides, we've got plenty of room. And," he added, "you know there's something else, as well. Since Buck quit, his house has just been standing empty." Frank shrugged. "It's behind the barn there and you could make it into your office.

See your clients in there and be right on-site to help Gracie out with this new business you're planning."

"That's a great idea, Dad," Emma said, and plucked Molly out of her high chair. Settling the baby on her hip, she looked at Gracie. "If you want, I'll give you two my bedroom, it's bigger."

"Seriously?" Gracie grinned at her sister.

"It sounds perfect," Madison said, looking at Gracie. "What do you think?"

"I think I love you and how soon can we pull this off?"

Madison laughed, jumped up and ran to the end of the table to hug Frank and kiss his cheek. "Thank you, Frank. This means so much."

Gracie was right behind her. "Thank you, Dad."

He patted both of them. "You girls are going to give me lots of fun and keep this old house from being too quiet. It's a win-win for me."

"And me," Gracie said, looking at Madison. Stepping right up to her, she cupped Madison's face in her palms and kissed her with all the love she'd been hiding for too long.

Seeing the two women share in the joy of loving each other only made Emma realize just how much Caden meant to her and just how much she'd lost.

Over the next few days, Emma concentrated on her new job. Though Caden was continually on her mind, she forced herself to focus on the kids. Teaching them reminded her of what she'd loved about acting. The purity of stepping into a new role, becoming someone else for a while and understanding what drove that character.

And when she did that, she found herself imagining Caden and what was driving him. She knew that man better than anyone else in her life. They'd been together for years and always, until she left, they'd shared a view of what their lives would be like. Then when he began to talk about getting married, Emma had done a 180 on him.

Even as much as she'd loved him, the thought of *forever* had scared the hell out of her. Especially when she'd never been outside Montana. Never tried to do anything with the dreams that danced at the edge of her mind. So she'd walked away from the man who meant everything.

And when she did that, she'd destroyed something beautiful. Those years in California, Emma had been lonely and the longing for Caden was a physical ache that she carried with her every day. But now it was so much worse. She was home. She'd been with him again, reminded herself of what she'd once had and now she'd lost him again.

But she wasn't going to quit. She wouldn't leave and give him the satisfaction of saying, *See? I knew she wouldn't stay.* No. She'd be right here. Day in. Day out. Until he believed again. Trusted again. And if someone tried to take Molly from her, then she would run, straight to Caden, and ask him to stand with her. To fight with her.

He'd called her hardheaded? Well, he had no idea just how stubborn she could be.

The email arrived first thing Saturday morning.

When Emma saw the name of the sender, her heart gave a hard jolt. Mouth suddenly dry, palms damp, she clicked on it, read the two short sentences and knew she was in trouble.

Arriving this afternoon at three o'clock to retrieve my daughter. Be there.
Dorian Baxter

"The bluff didn't work," she murmured and swallowed back a wave of nausea. She was scared, but not surprised. She'd known this would happen. Dorian Baxter wasn't the kind of man to give up easily. With his money and power behind him, he steamrollered people who tried to stand against him.

She glanced over at the baby, lying on a quilt in the great room, kicking both legs and waving her arms in a golden slice of sunlight as if she were a cheerleader. Molly was *her* daughter now and nothing was going to change that.

"Don't you worry, sweetie. I won't let him have you. Ever."

"What happened?" Gracie came into the room, a worried frown carved into her features.

"Molly's father's coming today to take her."

"Well, screw that," Gracie blurted and Emma smiled, thankful for the support.

"Screw what?" Madison came in behind her.

Madison had moved most of her things into the house a few days ago. They were still working things out and settling in, but it was amazing how happy Gracie was now that she was free to be in love.

"That Hollywood bastard is coming to take Molly," Gracie said, then turned to Emma. "I told her all about it."

"Well, he can't have her," Madison said, instantly going to the baby and scooping her up off the floor. Holding her close, she looked at Emma. "Right?"

"Absolutely right," she agreed. "But we need a plan."

"You're not going to run, are you?" Gracie asked quietly.

Emma looked at her sister. When would it stop? she wondered. When would the people she loved stop expecting her to leave? She hadn't *run away* five years ago. She'd run *to* something. And a little more than a week ago, she'd done the same thing.

She'd run to Montana. To home. To family. To *Caden*.

"I'm not going anywhere," she said firmly, meeting Gracie's eyes to drive home the message.

"Of course she's not leaving," Madison said, gently swaying Molly from side to side. Looking at Emma, she asked, "What do we do?"

Emma smiled at her and felt a rush of affection

for the newest member of the family. She was turning into a great sister. "Thanks, Mad. What we're going to do is fight back. I have to call Caden. Tell him what's happening."

More nerves. She hadn't spoken to him since that awful day in his stables. When he'd told her he couldn't trust her. When he told her that what they had was over because he couldn't risk a relationship with her again.

But he'd also said that he would help her fight for Molly. Now, she told herself as she hit speed dial, she'd find out if he'd meant it or not.

At three o'clock on the nose, Dorian Baxter walked into Emma's house. And it felt like storm clouds sailed in with him. Tall and handsome, he was dressed in a perfectly tailored three-piece suit, and looked just what he was—rich, powerful, sure of himself.

Caden wasn't there. He'd told her he would be, but he hadn't arrived yet. Emma was facing the man down, and her family was there to support her. Frank, Molly and Madison ranged themselves behind her in sort of a defensive line. Madison was holding Gracie and giving Dorian a look that should have set fire to his hair.

"Is that her?" he asked abruptly.

"You don't know?" Emma countered, feeling her fury begin to rise to match the panic clawing at her insides. Molly's black hair and blue eyes were so much like Dorian's it's a wonder he had to ask.

He gave her a dismissive glance. "Why would I know? If that's her, get her ready to go. I assume you have a car seat for her? I'll need that for the drive to the airport."

"You can't have her," Frank said.

One dark, expertly shaped eyebrow lifted. "And you are?"

"Frank Williams. This is my place and that baby's not going anywhere."

Dorian merely shifted his gaze back to Emma. "I don't have time for this. You will hand over my daughter or I will have the sheriff out here to arrest you for kidnapping."

"Then that's what you'll have to do," Emma said, and hoped she sounded braver than she felt at the moment. She didn't want to go to jail. She didn't have the money to fight Dorian in court. But there was simply not a chance in the world that she would give Molly to the man who had driven her mother to suicide.

The great room was big, comfortable and right now had sunlight filtering through the big window. Dorian looked as out of place in her home as she had in Hollywood.

Molly began to fuss as if she knew what was going on and Madison jiggled her to keep her quiet.

Dorian never took his eyes off Emma. "If you don't hand her over, I'll tell the police you threatened me with untrue, salacious stories. Attempted extortion."

"You don't want to do that," Emma said. "If that got into the news—and it would—you'd have to spend all of your time defending your reputation."

"I can kill the story."

"Before it damages you?" Because she knew as well as he did that his name would still be splashed across websites and headlines across the country. Even if he could prove later that she had been bluffing, he would have been ruined.

He shot his cuffs, tugged at his lapels and said, "Very well. We'll try this another way."

Worry jittered through Emma and she wondered where the hell Caden was. Why wasn't he here, standing beside her? Had he completely written her off now?

"What is it?" she asked, not really interested in his plan, but she did need to stall, to give Caden more time to arrive.

"All right. The truth is," he acknowledged with a slight tip of his head, "there are rumors flying around Hollywood and I've received a tip from a reporter friend—"

Translation, Emma thought, *a reporter on his payroll...*

"There's going to be a story coming out soon that the baby's mother committed suicide and that someone is hiding the kid."

Emma's stomach tightened.

"So here's my final offer," Dorian said, ignoring everyone in the room but Emma. "I will put you in my next movie—a modern take on the classic Western—" He looked around and sniffed. "Seems you'd be uniquely qualified for the role. You would be the second lead. A jumping-off point for your career that most actresses would kill to be offered."

Emma took a breath and held it. "In exchange for?"

He smiled and gave the impression of a snake, opening its mouth to envelop its prey. "You sign a paper saying that I've been paying you to care for the kid and that I visited and blah, blah, blah…" He paused for effect. "You do that, and you're a star. Turn it down, and I'll destroy you."

The whole house got quiet as if everyone in the room had taken a collective breath in anticipation of how Emma would handle this.

But for Emma, she was suddenly calm. She was being offered everything she used to dream about—and she didn't care. Whatever happened next, she knew Dorian had nothing she wanted. She wasn't interested in Hollywood. Didn't trust Dorian. And she wouldn't let him anywhere near Molly.

"No thanks," she said.

He shook his head as if he hadn't heard her correctly. "I'm sorry?"

"I said no," she said firmly, so there'd be no mistake.

"I'll let you keep the kid," he tossed in as an added temptation.

"Why you—" Frank took a step toward him, but Emma held up one hand to keep her father back.

"You don't have anything I need or want," Emma said. "I have everything, right here. This place holds my dreams. My home. My family. My *daughter*. Caden."

"Caden?" Dorian repeated. "Who the hell is that?"

"I'm Caden," he announced as he walked into the room. Tall, gorgeous, wearing black jeans and boots with a dark green shirt and his heavy brown jacket. He took off his hat as he marched across the floor and tossed it onto the nearest table.

Emma's heart leaped up into her throat and tears welled in her eyes. She shouldn't have doubted him. Caden would always keep his word. He would always be there for her. When he walked up to her side and faced Dorian with her, Emma had never been happier.

"Ah, the cowboy hero," Dorian mused. "There's nothing you can do here. I've come for the kid and since Emma here won't make a deal, we're done."

"Not quite," Caden said, and reached into his jacket for a sheaf of papers. In an aside to Emma, he said, "Sorry I'm late. I had to go see Max first."

"What's this about?" Dorian demanded.

"This is about the investigators my attorney hired," Caden told him. "Seems we found several women ready and willing to come forward and testify against you for assault and harassment. And guess what? One of those women was underage when you went after her. In California, that's statutory rape."

"You rotten no good—" Frank muttered it, but Gracie gave him an elbow nudge to quiet him.

"You're bluffing again," Dorian said, but he looked a bit less confident than he had a few minutes ago.

"Read it for yourself," Caden said and handed over the papers.

Emma looked up at him and Caden nodded, dropping one arm around her shoulder in support. She drew on his strength, curbed her curiosity and waited. For the first time since opening that email a few hours ago, she felt…hopeful.

Dorian scanned them, one after the other and Emma watched him pale. Lifting his gaze to Caden, ignoring Emma completely, he said only, "What do you want?"

Caden dipped into his pocket again and drew out a single sheet of paper. "I want you to sign this."

Eyes narrowed suspiciously, he demanded, "What is it?"

"Simple." Caden's lake-blue eyes were winter cold as he stared at the man. "You sign away all interest in the baby, releasing her to be adopted by Emma…or I give these statements to the press and you can kiss your freedom and your lifestyle goodbye."

Clearly furious, Dorian folded up the statements and tucked them into his suit jacket. Then he snatched the single sheet of paper from Caden, took a pen from his pocket and leaned over a table, scrawling his name across the bottom. When he was finished, he threw the paper back at Caden. "There. Our business is done?"

"Yes," Emma said, forcing him to look at her. To recognize her. "We're finished. You can leave, Mr. Baxter."

"With pleasure." He turned and stormed out of the house, slamming the front door behind him.

"Well, now," Frank said with admiration as he grinned at Caden. "I have an urge to open some windows and let the stink out. But that was the smoothest thing I've seen in years."

Caden smiled back. "I get the feeling that man's not used to losing. But he'll have to adapt soon enough."

"What? Why?" Emma asked. "He signed, it's over. But, Caden, would you really have released those statements?"

"Hell yes," he assured her. "To keep that baby away from a predator? You bet. But as it turns out, I won't have to. Instead, Max is faxing those statements to the LA police. I suspect they're going to have questions for Mr. Hollywood when he gets home."

Gracie laughed out loud, swept the baby out of Madison's arms and danced with her around the room. Mad kissed Caden's cheek and said, "Our hero."

"All right now, everybody into the kitchen. We'll

feed our baby and have a beer to celebrate!" Frank led the way and Gracie, Molly and Madison were right behind him.

"Thank you," Emma said when they were alone. She could hardly believe it was over. Molly was safe. And Caden was here, with her. All she had to do now was find a way to convince him to stay with her.

"I told you I'd be here for you and Molly, Em."

She looked up at him and thought Madison was right—he was a hero. But he hadn't done it for her. He'd done it for Molly. To keep that baby safe and in a loving family.

"And I told you, I wouldn't run. Not from you." Emma took a breath and said, "I'll never leave you again, Caden. I wish I could make you believe—"

"I do believe you," he said.

Shaken, Emma staggered a little. "You do? Why? Since when?"

"Because I heard you, Emma. Yeah, going to see Max slowed me down, but when I got here, I was in the foyer when that oily bastard offered you everything you left me for five years ago. I waited to see what you would say to stardom. A big movie. The dream." He lifted one hand to stroke his fingertips along her cheek. "And you said no. You chose me. You chose *us*."

"I'll always choose you, Caden," Emma said and blinked furiously to keep her tears at bay. She wanted to see him and didn't want a blur distracting from the sight of him looking down at her with love in his eyes.

"This is my home. My place. My dreams are here now." She smiled at him and said, "I love that job at the school. I'm going to be helping Mad and Gracie. Molly's going to grow up here knowing she's loved. And I'm not going anywhere. Why would I when everything I've ever wanted is right here?"

His mouth curved and that smile lit up his eyes. "I really do believe you, Emma. I trust you. And I love you more than I thought it was possible to love anyone."

Her heart swelled until she was sure it would simply burst out of her chest. "Then I've got something else to say to you, Caden Hale."

"Yeah?" Still smiling. Still loving her.

Slowly, Emma went down on one knee in front of him and he tried to pull her to her feet.

"Come on, Emma, get up."

"No." She looked up at him and saw everything she'd ever wanted in her life, shining in his eyes. "I know this isn't the usual way, and maybe I'm swallowing a little pride here, but I can do that. For you. For us. Caden, I'm asking you to marry me."

His eyes flashed and his jaw went tight.

"It's only fair that I be the one to propose because it was me who made such a mess out of things to begin with." She blinked back tears and hurried on. "I'm not sorry I went to California. But not for the reasons you might think. It's because being there, away from you, made me realize just how much you mean to me. You're everything, Caden. There are no dreams without you."

"Damn it, Emma, stand up now…"

"Not until I finish." She took another breath and kept her gaze fixed on his. "I want you to marry me. And love me. And adopt Molly with me and then make more babies with me. I want to live with you in that beautiful house and hunt for more gold with you, if you can find that vein again—"

He gave her wry smile. "Ha ha."

She grinned. "I want to help build that ranch of yours into the best in the state. Maybe in the country," she said and then added, "I love you, Caden, more than anything and now I want to know when you're going to say something!"

"Where's my ring?" he asked, smiling.

"Your ring?"

"Who proposes without a ring?"

Emma glared at him. "Are you kidding?"

"Yes." Grinning, Caden reached down and pulled her to her feet. "I was just waiting for you to run out of words." He took her face in his palms, looked into her eyes and said, "Yes, I'll marry you. I love you, Emma, now and forever. And if you ever need to run again, all you have to do is speak up and we'll run together."

Emma covered his hands with hers and felt as if she'd finally, completely, come home.

"I won't have to run, Caden. My world is right

here. My dreams are here. With you." She went up on her toes and kissed him, then said, "Who knows, maybe one of my students at the school will go off and take the world by storm. But as for me, the only storm I'm interested in is the one that happens between us whenever we touch."

"Then get ready, honey," he whispered, leaning down to kiss her. "There's a hell of a storm headed our way."

* * * * *

Meet more great ranching heroes from
USA TODAY *bestselling author Maureen Child!*

Rich Rancher's Redemption
Wild Ride Rancher
The Cowboy's Pride and Joy

All available now!

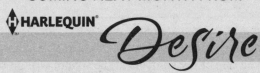

SPECIAL EXCERPT FROM

Gabe Dalton knows he should ignore his attraction to Jamie Dodge...but her tough-talking attitude masks an innocence that tempts him past breaking point...

Read on for a sneak preview of
Cowboy to the Core
by New York Times *and* USA TODAY
bestselling author Maisey Yates.

"You sure like coming up to me guns blazing, Jamie Dodge. Just saying whatever it is that's on your mind. No concern for the fallout of it. Well, all things considered, I'm pretty sick of keeping myself on a leash."

He cupped her face, and in the dim light he could see that she was staring up at him, her eyes wide. And then, without letting another breath go by, he dipped his head and his lips crushed up against Jamie Dodge's.

They were soft.

Good God, she was soft.

He didn't know what he had expected.

Prickles, maybe.

But no, her lips were the softest, sweetest thing he'd felt in a long time. It was like a flash of light had gone off and erased everything in his brain, like all his thoughts had been printed on an old-school film roll.

There was nothing.

Nothing beyond the sensation of her skin beneath his fingertips, the feel of her mouth under his. She was frozen beneath his touch, and he shifted, tilting his head to the side and darting his tongue out, flicking it against the seam of her lips.

She gasped, and he took advantage of that, getting entry into that pretty mouth so he could taste her, deep and long, and exactly how he'd been fantasizing about.

Oh, those fantasies hadn't been a fully realized scroll of images. No. It had been a feeling.

An invisible band of tension that had stretched between them in small spaces of time. In the leap of panic in his heart when he'd seen her fall from the horse earlier today.

It had been embedded in all of those things and he hadn't realized exactly what it meant he wanted until the right moment. And then suddenly it was like her shock transformed into something else entirely.

She arched toward him, her breasts pressing against his chest, her hands coming up to his face. She thrust her chin upward, making the kiss harder, deeper. He drove his tongue deep, sliding it against hers, and she made a small sound like a whimpering kitten. The smallest sound he'd ever heard Jamie Dodge make.

He pulled away from her, nipped her lower lip and then pressed his mouth to hers one more time before releasing his hold.

She looked dazed. He felt about how she looked.

"I thought about it," he said. "And I realized I couldn't let this one go. I let you criticize my riding, question my authority, but I wasn't about to let you get away with cock-blocking me, telling me you're jealous and then telling me you don't know if you want me. So I figured maybe I'd give you something to think about."

Don't miss
Cowboy to the Core *by Maisey Yates,*
available July 2019 wherever
Harlequin® books and ebooks are sold.

www.Harlequin.com

PHMYEXP0719